THE KEY ABOVE THE DOOR

Maurice Walsh was born at Balydonahue, Kerry, in 1879, the son of a farmer, and educated at St Michael's College, Listowel. For the first twenty years of this century he worked in the British Civil Service, after which he was in the Irish Free State Service. He had a great love for the Scottish Highlands and was a friend of Neil Gunn. He was the author of adventure and detective stories as well as stories about Ireland. He died in 1964.

By the same author in Pan Books

THE SMALL DARK MAN

THE KEY
ABOVE THE DOOR

MAURICE WALSH

UNABRIDGED

PAN BOOKS LIMITED : LONDON

First published 1926 by W. & R. Chambers Ltd.
This edition published 1973 by Pan Books Ltd,
33 Tothill Street, London, SW1.

ISBN 0 330 23494 3

2nd Printing 1973

Printed and bound in England by
Hazell, Watson & Viney Ltd,
Aylesbury, Bucks

FOREWORD

If, lured by the opening prospect of ben and corrie, you venture wheel on the old military road that runs tortuously from the highlands of the Dee to the great rift of Glenmore, you will ultimately come, under the favour of Providence, into a very welter of hills – brown and gently rolling – at the top end of the Province of Moray, and discover Loch Ruighi shining in its hollow.

It is not a large sheet of water – three miles in length by less than half that in width – and the whole expanse of it can be taken in at a glance. That glance will be early drawn to the ruined walls of the Wolf of Badenoch's stronghold, thrusting themselves out of the water near mid-loch; and, if you know the facts, you may muse for a space on the remarkable career of that royal old robber-baron. Presently, on the western side of the loch, your wandering eye will rest – gladly, because of the contrast – on two or three green fields like an oasis in the wastes of heather, and the white gleam of a crofter's dwelling will shine at you through a clump of willows near the water. Within the upheaved horizon – brown moor lifting over brown moor – no other habitation of man is apparent; yet, if you know where to look, a keen scrutiny will reveal one on the eastern side of the loch. It is a squat cottage with walls and thatch toning exactly with the heather and the outcropping of limestone, and it nestles on the sunny side of Cairn Rua, halfway between the shining water of the loch and the sombre green pinewood crowning the hill. That cottage is the seasonal abiding place of one Thomas King – Tom King of Loch Ruighi – who will set things before you in the following pages.

You are likely enough to meet Tom King on the road that curves with the eastern shore of the loch on any day from July to October; and, should it be necessary to inquire a way out of these fastnesses, you will find him very ready to talk. You will notice that he has a quaint and frank turn of speech, and, if you have a bent that way, he will lead you into queer and original byways of discussion, so that at the end of half an hour, or even an hour, you will go on your way wondering if this tall, lean, youngish man in the careless tweeds, with the masked face and the live eyes, is really the moorland crofter he professes to be.

If you are one of those lucky ones who, not troubled by the consideration of ways and means, migrate, say, to the south of Spain in October, you may again run across Tom King, still in his loose tweeds, lazying in the sunny gardens of Seville, or loitering down the long valley of the Madura, where the white houses are strung along the river. He will know you at once, and, if you prove yourself of the elect, he will almost certainly introduce you to one or two dark cellars, beneath the white house, where the amber wines of that country are maturing in tall brown jars.

You will then know that Tom King is no moorland crofter. Later on you may be tempted to call him an egotist: the egotist that the natural man always is. Ultimately you will discover that he is, quite simply and without pose, a compound of gentleman and tramp, hermit and wanderer, scholar and ignoramus, realist and idealist, and of many other things as well — in short, a seeker of beauty and a believer in the dominion of reason over imagination.

Out of his natural egotism, his unreasoning adherence to pure reason, and the real live manhood in him arises this tale.

CHAPTER I

I, Thomas King of Loch Ruighi, will begin this narrative with a relation of the events that befell me – and my friends – on a July day in the Province of Moray. I could begin a long way farther back than that and tell of the circumstances, the chances, the predilections, the little side-winds that made me forsake the wandering paths of the world and anchored me loosely to a hermit's life in a stone bothy on the limestone breast of Cairn Rua, above the shining waters of Loch Ruighi. That telling might be a nice exercise in self-diagnosis, but it would be no more than a long-winded introduction to the gist of my story; moreover, as I go on, there will be more than enough opportunity for self-diagnosis, which is one of my vices and the worst form of egotism.

Therefore I will begin the day on which I first met Agnes de Burc. On that day Neil Quinn out of Ireland, and Alistair Munro out of Sutherland, came across the hills from Inverness in a side-car outfit, and the three of us spent the forenoon trying to catch a mess of trout in Loch Ruighi. We caught none. The loch was as still as a splash in a rut, and the silver of it was dulled with a tenuous, shimmering heat-haze, whilst overhead arched a brazen July sky, flecked here and there with the whitest of cloud. I often wonder whether it was the hopelessness of the fishing or the prompting of my own destiny that made me suggest an expedition across the moor to the Leonach River. Whichever it was, the afternoon found us plodding up the long slope of Aitnoch Hill, and sagging down among the scattered birches of the Leonach Glen. In that glen destiny had me safely in its trap.

Through untold antediluvian centuries the curbed Leonach fretted a channel deeper and deeper into the red-brown sandstone of its bed, until it reached the stubborn mother-basalt, and deeper than that it has not yet gone. It is not as limestone clear as the White Avon of Upper Banff, nor as sternly impetuous as the mighty Spey, nor as swift as the rock-torn

Findhorn, but the pale amber of it running serenely over its basalt ledges between its high, birch-grown, ruddy sandstone bluffs makes it one of the bonniest rivers in all the north. Let me make it clear here and now that it was that beauty and its quietness that drew us across the four miles of moor from Loch Ruighi. The thought of poaching never entered our heads. In the first place, I had no need to poach the Leonach. My friend and landlady, Mary, Lady Clunas, owned that countryside, and I got all the fishing I cared for under the good-natured surveillance of Davy Thomson, her head keeper. And yet, that day fate drove us to try in mere curiosity one of the poacher's favourite methods. This was the way of it.

We came down on the Leonach at the head of Dalbuie Pool, and the moment Munro saw the amber clearness of it he exclaimed, 'My heavens! What a river to poach!'

He was a rascally Highlandman from the borders of Caithness, and the pools of the Dunbeath River knew him but too well. His remark set us talking of the many ways, besides the legal ones, of taking salmon.

'In low water and under a sky like yon,' said Munro, 'there is only one way of catching a fish honestly.'

'He has all a good man's parts and honesty besides,' quoted the Irishman. 'Is it a stick of gelignite or a long-handled gaff you'd be thinking of?'

'Too obvious! I would use a staff with a loop of brass wire at the end of it.'

'G'wan,' scoffed the Irishman. 'Rabbits you have in your mind.'

'I could show you. There's Tom King's hazel staff, and you have an old salmon-trace round your hat. You show me a fish under a ledge in three or four feet of water, and I'll show you how to snare him out by the tail.'

Quinn looked at me with a speculation in his dark eye.

'I would like to see the lad try it,' he said softly.

'It can be done,' I told him, 'but, besides being sinful, it is daylight poaching.'

'Even the just man falls seven times a day.'

'Moreover,' I went on, faintly protesting, 'these fishings and shootings have recently been let by Lady Clunas, and the new

8

tenant and his party are just arrived at Reroppe Lodge at the other side of Tomlachlan Knoll yonder. If they come on us—'

'If they are fishermen,' interrupted Munro, 'they will be giving the river a rest on a day like this.'

There and then I fell.

'Very well,' I said; ' 'tisn't likely you'll be doing much harm. Come with me, and I'll show you where a fish lies; and, if Davy Thomson catches us, our fates be on our own heads.'

We went on down the course of the stream. Half the river-bed was dry, and the water was no more than a chain of pools strung on singing shallows that were pleasantly cool above our brogue-tops as now and again a jutting bluff forced us to splash across. On either hand the sandstone banks rose high and sheer, and above them were steep slopes grown with larch and pine – a pattern of bright and dark green – whilst over all arched the white-flecked sky, full of lazy, warm afternoon light. We felt little and remote and safe down there in the wide gut of the hills.

In time we came to the great Poul na Bo, the biggest pool in all the upper reaches of the Leonach: forty yards in width, very deep and dark under the bluffs opposite us, but shallow-ing steadily to the middle, where a ridge of basalt stood well out of the water. On the near side of that ridge the pool was then in no place deeper than a foot or two, and it shallowed to a few inches bordering the gravelly spit on which we stood.

'Now then, Highlandman,' I told Munro, 'the time has come to prove your skill – and then for home, fish or no fish. Myself, I do not usually poach Davy Thomson's territory. Wait till I fix your noose for you. There you are. See you that ledge yonder in mid-pool? That's your stance. You'll find at least one salmon on the other side and close under it.'

'How am I to get there?'

'You'll wade – 'tisn't deep, and the water is warm.'

'Ay, faith!' cried Quinn, his fingers already at his shoe-laces. 'I am coming too.'

I filled a pipe and, as they waded towards the ledge of basalt, admired the long sinewy legs of the Irishman and the sturdy props of his companion, and so clear was the amber water through which they moved that I could see the refracted ivory blur of their feet feeling for smooth going on the rock bottom. It was about then that I had the first telepathic twinge. To my mind came very strongly the knowledge that I could no longer claim the privileges that were mine when Lady Mary kept the fishings in her own hands. The new tenant might, and indeed would, resent any infringement of his rights. Though we were only playing at poaching, still, poaching we actually were – and using, at that, one of the favourite methods of the experienced and cunning professional.

Some instinct urged me to recall the lads, but I hesitated until too late. Already they were lying across the ledge and peering cautiously over and down. Followed a little pause, and then, from the sudden stiffening of their sprawling legs, it became clear that they had marked a fish. They drew back, gave me a nod of head and a twist of thumb, edged along into position, and forthwith Munro began the stealthy manipulation of his noosed staff.

CHAPTER II

Poul na Bo makes no sound, so big and deep is it, and so far away round the curve of the shore are the shallows at its foot. That is why I heard so distinctly the clink of an iron-shod shoe while its wearer was still out of sight beyond the out-jutting bluff down-stream. That small, clinking sound startled me very thoroughly, for in my then state of mind any strange footstep portended danger. Not for all the clean fish in the Leonach would I have my two young friends in trouble. They were in a rotten position strategically. I dared not cry out to them to slip out of sight on the far side of the ridge, and indeed they, oblivious of everything but their fish, must even now be fully visible to whoever walked on shore.

My lips were framed for a warning whistle, when, by some freak of luck or skill, Munro succeeded in noosing and holding his fish. Followed a loud splash, a writhing of bare legs, a gleam of silver as the fish threshed on the ledge, and shouts of triumph as the lads pounced on it. And quick as an echo to their shouts came a stentorian bellow from the shore. I was startled – so startled that I suffered confusion of thought. If in that crisis I had stood my ground it is probable that we could have got out of our scrape with a little unpleasantness but without disaster. But at the moment the only clear idea that came to me was that I must remain unseen and retain freedom of action until I found out what we had to face. On that idea I acted promptly.

Luckily, the bank behind me had broken down to masses of rock grown with stunted birches. Just behind me was a huge and almost detached mass of stone with the crown of a birch tree leaning conveniently over it. For no clean-cut reason, but for two or three jumbled ones, I swept the lads' shoes and hose into a bundle, and, tucking it under my arm, scrambled up the angle between rock and bank, ducked under the screen of birch, and lay flat.

Things were moving at their own pace down below. A shouting, angry beyond question, reverberated from bank to bank, and not one pair of feet but many crunched the gravel. Where I lay nothing could be seen but the pale backs of the heart-shaped birch leaves with little points of sunlight between, and at all risks I must see what was toward. I hitched forward on my elbows until I could look over the edge of the rock and through the screen of leaves.

First I saw my friends sitting on the ridge in mid-pool, their feet in the water and the blasted salmon between them. They struck some depraved humorous note in me with their white-gleaming bare legs asprawl and their heads alert – a queer compound of carelessness and astonishment. Their gaze was fixed on the shore directly below me, and I hitched myself forward another inch and peeped down.

'Great horn spoon!' I said below my breath. 'The whole sheep this time.'

On the edge of the pool, ten feet beneath me, stood two men, who could be none other than the new people at Reroppe, and at their backs were all their myrmidons: Davy Thomson the head keeper, two gillies weighted with all the paraphernalia of the salmon-fisher, and a fourth man in the serf-garb of a chauffeur. Protruding from a fishing-bag on the back of one of the gillies was the broad tail of a salmon, and oddly enough I found time to wonder by what lure that fish had been caught on such a day of stillness and sun. A gleam of white drew my eyes down-stream to where a lady stood at gaze, just within the point of the out-jutting bluff. The only impression I had time to gather was that she was young and tall, and that her face was turned steadily on the squatters in mid-stream. The stage was fully set, and already I was wondering whether I was fated to be audience only.

One of the gentlemen, his shoe-toes actually in the water, gestured with a not-to-be-denied authority. 'Come out of it, damn you! Come on out of it!' he shouted in a great, angry voice.

He was a big man, with high, massive shoulders, a splendid column of neck that does not usually go with such shoulders, and a bare, round, sleek, blue-black head.

The unfortunates sat calmly on their rock, and looked at each other. They seemed to be calculating their plight with some coolness. They looked up the stream and down the stream, and back over their shoulders at the high wall of rock hemming them in. Some words passed between them, and then side by side they slipped into the water and slowly waded in towards the now silent group on the shore. They had decided to face the music. The Irishman trailed the dead salmon by the tail, and on his lean face was a twisted grin. Munro's brows were drawn down in a stiff bar; his mouth was shut like a trap; and in all the subsequent flurry he said very little, and that little bluntly.

I found my heart beating a little quickly and emptily. I could not see how the predicament might work out harmlessly, and I refused to contemplate disaster. It was clear enough, however, that whatever ensued, only one of two courses would be open to me. If the lads had decided to give nothing away, then my part was to remain a free agent and be ready to give help when help might be useful. If, on the other hand, they had decided to make a clean breast of it, then I must come into the open and do what could be done. I saw no third course, and so, while the lads waded slowly across the pool, while yet I had time to reason, I decided to choose one course or the other in accordance with my friends' decision.

Neil Quinn, halting in a few inches of water, was first to speak. 'We have been catching your fish for you, anyway,' he said calmly.

'And your authority?' queried the big man just as calmly, but one felt that the held-coolness of his voice cloaked a deep sense of outrage.

'Faith! 'tis doubtful,' said the Irishman whimsically, 'and we were fools to trust it.'

'You knew you were poaching?'

'Of course we did,' put in Munro bluntly, and spoiling all chance Quinn might have had of lightening the issue with his nimble Irish tongue.

The big man said no word for an appreciable time. Then he turned quickly and addressed the man who was standing a little behind him on his right. As he turned his head I caught a glimpse of his black-browed, strong-jawed face.

'What is the worst we can do to the whelps?' he questioned.

'That is a jolly nice fish they've got,' said his friend, in such an easy tone that my gaze was drawn to him. He was a very tall and thin man in loose tweeds, and he carried his hands deep in his trouser pockets.

'Aweel, Mr Leng,' broke in old Davy Thomson, stumping forward, 'the dom scutts hae no richt on oor water. For ae thing we can be chasin' them off it.'

'I'll do a darn sight more than that,' said his employer grimly. 'What is the law in the matter?'

'Ye can hae an interdict tae haud 'em frae fishin'—'

'Fishing! Call that fishing!' cried the other, pointing to where the dead salmon lay in the shallows still attached to my noosed staff.

'And a mighty neat method too,' remarked the thin man.

'Fit I was coming at, Mr Leng,' said Davy, 'was that thae loons hae been takkin' fish by illegal practices, an' that's a jailin' job, as they ken fine.'

'How some of us do cheat the gaol!' said the thin man laughingly, and Davy grinned sheepishly.

13

'Tut! Tut! Murray,' cried the big man impatiently. 'You should know my rights.'

'You can sue them for damages, I suppose.'

'Ay, and for poachin' and foul fishin' as weel, Mr Leng,' added Davy, who did not love poachers.

'Do you know them, Thomson?' questioned Leng.

' 'Deed no, but I can aye be findin' oot.'

'I shall find out right now, by the Lord!' cried Leng, and he swung with insolent confidence on the lads, who, during this discussion, had been standing quietly in the ankle-deep water.

'I will take that fish and your names as well,' he ordered in a tone expecting no refusal.

'The fish surely,' said Quinn, stepping out of the water and laying the salmon on the gravel. 'The fish because it is yours.'

'Your names too?'

'Our names are our own,' said Quinn, and he straightened his lean, wiry length and looked the big man in the eye.

'Damn you, sir!' cried the other. 'I'll have your name.'

' 'Tis a great pity, indeed,' said Quinn regretfully, 'that a small lack of humour is for spoiling a fine day at the end of it.'

The Irishman was calm as a post and wholly unashamed. His face was neither set like Munro's nor twisted into its customary half-cynical smile; it was a very still face only, and gave no hint of what moved below it. Leng, the big man, might have seen by now that browbeating this lad was a hopeless task, but by this time Leng had become too irate to exercise reason or prudence. 'By Heaven, sir!' he threatened, 'if you do not disclose your name I'll shake it out of you.'

Forthwith he thrust out a strong hand, gripped Quinn roughly by the shoulder, gave him a contemptuous shake, and jerked him forward.

And Quinn, as he came forward, hit the big man a thundering upward blow in the face and stretched him his length on the gravel.

The sudden explosion of that blow showed that the Irishman had all this time been trying to hold down his mounting native temper. All that suppression was loosed in his right arm, and Leng went down as if his legs had been snatched from under him. I did not expect him to rise for some time, but underestimated the force and fibre of the man; for he came to his feet like a rubber ball, and with the voiceless grunt of the true fighting animal was about to hurl himself on Quinn, when the cool Mr Murray interposed.

Already I was crouching on my knees for the spring that would land me amongst them, when Murray's quick action made me pause in that pose. That action was prompt and decisive. As Leng was in the act of thrusting himself forward, Murray caught him under the arm, and, by some remarkable trick of skill or strength, swung him half round and held him so. Leng swore sharply, glared, and made to drag his arm away.

'Easy, Leng, easy!' said Murray in his calm voice. 'Let us pause for a moment.'

Quite suddenly, and by a remarkable and visible effort of will, the big man calmed down. It was as if Murray's quiet words had shown him things from a new and more dignified angle.

'All right, Murray!' he said steadily. 'Let me deal with this.'

He loosed his arm without brusqueness and turned to Quinn, and again I eased myself down and watched. Up to the present things had developed too quickly for me. It was increasingly difficult now to remain a mere onlooker. But at the same time things had come to such a pass that my appearance on the scene could not avert any action contemplated by the irate Mr Leng. Therefore, outside all angry urge, it was my plain duty to wait, and act only when action would help. That duty I must abide by.

The big man leant towards Quinn and spoke into his face, but he kept his hands to himself, and his bullying manner had altered to settled determination. 'You will give me your name?'

'Is the information important?'

His calm was back on Quinn, but his expanded nostrils and steadfast eyes showed how ready he was for action.

'You'll find it important, I promise,' said the other grimly.

He must have seen that questioning was useless, for without further pressing he turned to his friend. 'I will never let them go now, Murray,' he cried.

'Your pidgin,' said Murray. 'I will stay with you.'

15

But old Davy Thomson was beginning to be troubled. Like the doughty poacher-fighter he was, he knew something of the law, and did not want his employer to act so high-handedly as to prejudice his case. 'If you'll be leaving them in my hands, Mr Leng,' he said, 'they'll no' be finding it easy to gang free o' this snarl.'

'Leave this to me, Thomson,' said his employer curtly. 'In the first place, we'll take them to Reroppe, and, if they remain recalcitrant, we'll run them down to Forres after dinner, and let the police deal with them.'

'Better let them get their footgear on,' suggested Murray.

At that I drew back my head and lay very still. Any half-thorough search would find the footgear. In my then mood I did not greatly mind if they did find the footgear and a Tartar.

'Where are your shoes?' I heard Leng ask.

There was no reply, and I ventured another peep. Quinn and Munro were looking speculatively at each other. The old twisted smile flitted across the Irishman's face. 'What for would two wild Hielan'men be wanting brogans on a day like this, whatever?' he said, with the true Gaelic accent.

'Where are your shoes?' Leng's voice was again rising.

'You are an obstinate devil,' said Quinn in his Irish tongue. 'I would not like to be you this day or any day, God help me!'

'They are aul' hands at the game,' put in Davy Thomson. 'We maun hae a look for the sheen; they'll no' be far awa'.'

'No, by the Lord!' cried Leng with emphasis. 'There will be no searching. We will take them just as they are, if they will have it so.'

'Carry on,' said Murray. 'I am not much in love with this work, but I suppose we must stay with it to a finish.'

There followed a pause – a pause queerly tense. Quinn and Munro stood with downcast eyes, and I knew that they were waiting for what I might do. I did nothing. And then the Irishman turned to his companion. 'The ploy is only begun, my son,' he said. 'We will just gang.'

'Very well,' agreed Munro quietly.

They had put their fate in my hands, and I must not fail them.

CHAPTER III

The strip of gravel was empty. From round the curve of the shore came the crunch of departing footsteps. I lay still till that sound died away, and, as I lay, concentrated my thoughts on things as they stood and as they might stand. At last I got to my knees, made a parcel of shoes and hose, tucked it under my arm, and beat from under the screen of birch leaves. And, straightening up, I found myself face to face with the lady in white: that lady in white of whom I had caught a glimpse before yet the issue was locked, and who had been ignored and forgotten, characteristically enough, by us males in our little war. She must have moved up the bank as things developed, and now she stood amongst the boulders directly behind my hiding-place. She was very cool-looking and unmistakably patrician in her white dress, and I was not cool at all. Probably my mouth gaped as I stared at her.

'I have been looking at your shoe-heels for quite a time,' she said almost casually, and at once I noticed the low-pitched timbre of her voice.

I looked down at my old brogues and back at her, and then at the rim of sandstone outside the birch fronds, and below that, and to the right, I could see the trampled gravel. That gave me an opening. 'Did you enjoy the war, madam?' I asked her.

'It was not a nice affair,' she gave me back, 'but a third man might have made it nicer.'

The ever-so-little bleak note of contempt in her voice silenced me, and disturbed me too.

She was a tall young woman and slim, and her white – or very light-cream – dress had something robe-like about it. She wore an oldish panama-hat, and her black hair peeped below it. There was little or no colour in her face, which was of that type of beauty that, in a travail of expression, we call proud, magnetic, electric, tragic; sombre, I think, is the best word of all, and the quality it attempts to describe is always in beauty of the highest quality: beauty of the calm, lean kind, dark-eyed and serious, proud and self-willed, fateful and unafraid, and made for love and desolation since Troy fell: beauty that fate plays with for its own ends, and that man has been thrall to since passion's first stir.

It seems to me now that, at my first glance, I could not help thus finally summing up that woman and her beauty. But, of course, all I could have noticed was that she was of aristocratic mould, and dowered with good looks and calmness.

'You have the rest of their clothes too,' she said, and her tone was again casual.

'So I have,' I said; 'and, if you will pardon me, I will be making shift to dispose of them.' I was about to turn away when a thought came to me. 'Madam,' I said, 'if you may want to get back to Reroppe your best road is over the bank up there, and to the right of the wooded knoll you will see facing you.'

I suggested that road, hoping that she would choose it instead of the path by the river. Her friends, expecting to find her somewhere on that path, would surely send back a gillie when they reached their car. I had no hope that she would remain silent. All I wanted was a little extra time, and, given that, was prepared to risk her speech – or anything else.

I lifted my old tweed hat and swung away to scramble up over the sandstone rocks above us. I did not spare myself in that climb, and in less than a minute was over the brow on a damp slope grown with black alders. Without a pause I slanted across this until, breaking through a bed of willows, I came out on the open moor; and there I stopped to get my wind and take my line. Right and left the moors spread and rolled and lifted into limestone-ribbed hills; in front of me rose a tufted knoll, and behind it, I knew, was the lodge of Reroppe. I chose the left flank of that knoll for my road, because, though rougher, it was the shorter – and then set out at a long swinging trot meant to cover a mile of old heather in as near five minutes as I could make it. I was running a race, and the men I must beat had to cover half a mile on foot and a mile by motor. There was no time to waste; but I was not yet old, and my fibre was mature, and the errand that moved me moved

18

me strongly. At no time did I see myself losing that race.

At the back of Reroppe Lodge is a long belt of dark pines, planted closely to keep off the snell north winds, and one coming in off the moors remains invisible from the lodge or the road approaching it. I got safely into that belt and through to its outer edge, where I threw myself flat behind a juniper bush and panted. The lodge with its outbuildings is shaped like the letter L and the sheltering pine-belt is parallel to the short arm and less than twenty paces away. Peeping from behind the juniper, I looked through a sagging wire fence directly across at the gun-room window, and well to the left of that I looked slantwise through the open back-door of Davy Thomson's byre. The byre would be empty I knew, for on the moor I had passed Davy's polled cow. In the doorway an old and broody hen complained crooningly, and I startled her as I darted across the open and into the byre. She went between my legs with a squawk and disappeared round the corner, clamouring outrageously. If any folks heard, I hoped they would blame some marauding stoat.

I pushed the door to behind me, and, though the front door was closed, enough light came through the chinks to show where a ladder, nailed perpendicularly against the end partition, gave access to the hayloft. I scrambled up this ladder into the loft, dropped the trap-door noiselessly, and found myself in darkness. This did not trouble me greatly, for I knew the internal economy of the lodge and its curtilages. The hayloft in which I stood ran the whole length of the outbuildings, the ground floor of which comprised a storeroom, byre, and what was once a stable. The stable, to suit the new civilization, was now converted into a motor garage, and had a big double-door broken in at the gable-end.

I silent-footed down the loft until I was above the garage. Here, instead of petrol, I smelled the fragrance of new-mown hay and shuffled forward until I came to where a small pile of it was heaped at the very end of the loft, near the door in the gable-end through which it had been forked. A chink or two of light came through the planking of this door and gave me my bearings. I looked for and found the trap-door opening directly over the disused stable manger. It was secured by a slip-through bolt which I gently drew, only to find that I could not lift the flap. By prising it at the corners I found that it was not nailed down, but secured below by another bolt. Satisfied on this point, I slipped the top bolt home and went back to the pile of hay, where I seated myself and waited.

'Now,' I thought to myself, 'I'll soon see if I have succeeded in thinking another man's thoughts.'

There was not long to wait. The purr of a motor came to me as it turned into the drive from the high-road, and its movements were easy to follow, as it slowed down, accelerated, reversed, and finally backed up to the garage door. Followed many sounds, and then the double-doors creaked open and the voice of the big man came through the floor. 'In there, you young whelps!' he said sternly. 'You'll speak when you are next spoken to – or take the consequences.'

There was a pause, and Leng again spoke. 'Is that trap-door secured from above, Thomson?'

'There is a guid bolt haudin' it onywey, Mr Leng,' came Davy's voice.

Someone scrambled on the manger, snicked back the lower bolt, and thumped forcefully on the trap-door. Thank the Lord that I had slipped the top bolt home.

'Quite secure,' said Leng. 'Come along, Murray, and let's eat. Howard' – this to the chauffeur – 'you sit in the car and watch that door. If there's any attempt to break out, blow your horn.'

The big double-doors clanged, footsteps receded over the cobbled yard, and in a little time there was silence. I was congratulating myself on my reasoning, when the silence was broken by the Irishman's voice. 'Surely a hectic hour, Alec!' he said.

'It is our move next,' said Munro, 'and we are up against it if we do not make it a good one.'

'I would be feeling twice a better man,' said Quinn, 'if I had something on my feet. Foundered beyond repair, and I've lost all delight in the simple life. I wonder what long Tom King of Loch Ruighi did with our togs?'

'I don't quite understand that long man of yours,' said Munro.

'He don't quit easily,' the Irishman upheld me. 'At the back o' my mind I hang on to him. 'Ssh!'

At that point I had leant forward and tapped the floor with my knuckles. There was a dead silence below. I started to crawl across the floor, tapping as I went. When I reached the trap-door I tapped that a little more loudly, eased back the bolt, and listened. The lads understood at once. Hardly had I withdrawn the bolt when the snick of the lower one reached me. The trap-door was pushed up beneath my hands, and the loft was no longer dark. The Irishman was standing on the ledge of the manger and peering up at me.

'Quick! You long devil,' I urged, and, catching his outstretched hand, had him in the loft in one clean lift. Munro followed with the agility of a monkey.

'Pleased to make your acquaintance, Mr King,' greeted Quinn. 'Did you come by broomstick?'

I slipped back to the hay-pile and fumbled for the parcel of shoes and hose. 'Here!' I whispered over my shoulder. 'Kick these on somehow, and hurry for the sake of your immortal souls.'

And they surely hurried. A groan or two as shoes pressed on lacerated feet, a whip-round of tangled laces, a muffled shamble down the loft, and in less than a minute we were down in the byre and at the back door.

'Do you see that plantation over there?' I pointed out. 'That is our first objective. Follow—'

Munro caught my arm, and his face was lighted as with a new thought. 'Wait you, long man!' he said.

'Don't be a silly young ass,' I reproved him testily, but he only gripped tighter.

'This ploy is not over yet,' he whispered. 'Will you tell me how the road runs from this place to where we left our motor-bike on your side of the loch?'

'Man-alive! that is not your road now—'

'Not *your* road. Can you not answer me?' and he shook my arm.

'To the right beyond the gates here, and in three miles the left fork round the south end of the loch.'

He dropped my arm and caught Quinn's. 'Neil,' he said, 'we

must get away quickly from this territory.' He jerked a thumb over his shoulder . . . 'What do you say?'

'Think of me forgetting that, Alistair boy!' said Quinn, grinning delightedly. He slapped me on the shoulder. 'This is no place for you, Tom King. We shall meet again, but now you must make your own road in the heather. This thing we are doing is due to us. Come along, Munro, let's take a peep anyway.'

It was so clear that any words of mine would be useless that I did not delay any longer in securing my own retreat. 'To hell with you!' I said, and made a slanting dash for the plantation, ducked below the wires, and flattened out. Lifting my head, I could see only the high bonnet of the car round the end of the garage, and I wormed sideways behind the junipers until the chauffeur came into my field of vision. He was sitting aside and carelessly on his seat, smoking a contemplative cigarette, one hand thrown over the back-rest and his eyes on the distant hills: an easy-minded, menial man, wholly unaware of the grievous evil creeping up on him. I was the sole observer of the brace of young tigers glaring at him from the gable corner, the sole spectator of the charge they made on him. He, poor victim, was startlingly plucked, like a rabbit, through the open door of the car, flapped on his face like a squab of mud, and held flat and helpless under the Irishman's knee.

Munro hopped into the driving-seat and dealt with levers boldly. There followed the metallic pulse of the self-starter, the purr of the engine taking on, the reckless acceleration, the check and catch of the too sudden clutch, and the jerk forward of the car. And then the Irishman gave his victim one final and reprehensible bump, and hurled himself over the lowered hood into the back seat. I saw his badly-laced shoes disappear as the car rocked and swerved into the drive.

The ensuing clamour had no attractions. I did not wait for it. I crawled down the fence behind the clumps of broom and juniper till, getting well on the blind side of the lodge, I made a crouching retreat through the spindly firs to the open moor, where I took to my heels in dead earnest, and never cried halt until I reached the shelter of the hollow in which flows the Rhinver Burn. By that little water I rested and chuckled with the stream, until I minded, with the least touch of chagrin, that a young woman in white knew more of my movements that day than I should like any woman to know.

'I wonder,' I mused, 'what use she will be making of her knowledge. Will she be forthright or will she play a woman's game? Praises be, I am not amenable to the games that women play!'

And with that smug thought I was about to rise to my feet, when a gleam of white caught my eye. I looked up, startled, for I suppose my nerves were still rather on edge. The lady of my thoughts was looking down at me from the head of the few feet of slope at the other side of the stream. A tall, slim lady in white, with the setting sun shining ruddily on her. She carried her old panama in her hand, and, though her black hair curled close to her head and to her white brow, a little wisp here and there was filmed against the glow of the evening sky. I noted all that before rising to my feet, and I was not long in doing that.

The half-cynical mood in which I had been thinking left me cool enough. I lifted my old hat, and: 'You are taking the long road home, madam,' I said.

'I fear so,' said the lady calmly. She did not smile, nor did she put on the aloofness of the patrician caste. 'I crossed this brook farther down, and now that I want to cross it again without wet feet it will not let me.'

'It likes good company too,' I said; 'but you are not far from a crossing-place now. Let me show you.'

Without another word we went up the burn together, and the water gurgled to itself between us. She was silent, and I wanted to hear her talk.

'Round this curve here,' I said, 'there are stepping-stones, and a path going down between the tussocks to Reroppe. The folks down there might be wondering.'

'Hardly,' she told me. 'One of the men came back to look for me on the river-side, and I told him I was coming across country.'

I said nothing to that, but I wondered if that was all she had told him. And then I remembered that when I lay in hiding under the birch tree she might easily have given me away and had not done so. That made me wonder all the more; and as I wondered, we arrived where the water shouldered round the stepping-stones.

'Here we are, my lady,' I told her. 'Watch your feet, now! Here's a hand if you need it.'

Lightly her white shoes touched the smooth whinstones, and I withdrew my outstretched hand untouched. A little cool, faintly-perfumed breeze brushed by me.

'Thank you,' said the lady. She stood within two yards and looked at me. 'You have got rid of your parcel,' she said quietly. 'I hope your – friends got their shoes.'

'They had need of them, at any rate. You will be told things down at the lodge, madam, and be able to draw your own conclusions.'

'They may be unpleasant ones.'

'They may, indeed. As a friend of mine said, many a fine day is spoiled at the end of it.'

'Whose fault will it be?'

'Mine surely, of course. All the blame is mine.'

'You seem to have avoided it up to the present.'

Again there was the little bleak note of disapproval, and again it touched me.

'My fate will find me out,' I said. 'It seems to be in your hands, my lady, so permit me to inform you that my name is Tom King, and that I live at Loch Ruighi over the hill there.'

'Thank you,' she said. 'I will remember – if necessary'; and she looked at me with something new in her expression.

'Davy Thomson, your head keeper,' I went on, 'will tell you things about me which are mostly not true – but he is a decent man, all the same. I have a small cottage and a bit croft on the hill of Cairn Rua, and a goat called Suzanne – because of her nimbleness. I have a boat on the loch too – if you are interested in fishing?'

'Not the fishing I saw this afternoon.'

'Yet that was a nice fish your people caught today, but Davy's long-handled gaff would be apt to hurt the poor thing. What fly did you use on a day like this?' I knew that the fish in the gillie's bag had never been caught by a fly.

Her steady-gazing eyes did not even flicker. I tried her once more.

'We do outrageous things here in the North – sometimes, and some of the things we do or have to do or leave undone are not always understood by civilized people from the South, but in our own way we generally carry things to a sort of a conclusion – as you might find out when you get back to Reroppe.'

'I shall remember what you say,' said my lady. 'Good evening, and thanks.'

And so she left me – still a nameless and somewhat strange young woman. For a few seconds I watched her go, and then turned and stared at the water shouldering round the stepping-stones.

'That young woman,' I considered, 'has me in the hollow of her white hands – as she thinks. She will be a strange young woman if she does not tell that big black young fellow about me and the craven part I played. I hope she did not expect me to plead with her. It would not be safe to shelter behind a woman's silence – a woman's silence, indeed! We must just wait on events, young lady, and, if you are the woman I expect you are, we need not lose patience in waiting.'

And so I went homewards up the long slopes of heather. By the time I reached the head of Aitnoch Hill the splendid spread of moors before me was darkening with an infinite gentleness in the half-light, and Loch Ruighi, in its hollow, was shining with a clear silver light of its own. The grey bulk of the Wolf's Island and the grey-green ash trees among the castle ruins stood out against that shine to the last broken line and the last gnarled twig.

As I rowed across the loch the white moth came out, and the whole expanse of water was ringed with feeding fish. I had three rods in the boat – Quinn's, Munro's, and my own – but all desire for fishing had left me. Instead, I pulled steadily to the other shore, and there moored my little craft at its home-made pier. Just opposite was the pathway leading up through the heather to my cottage, and by the open gateway, where the road curves with the shore of the loch, I looked for my friends' side-car outfit. It was not there, of course, nor was there any trace of the commandeered motor-car.

'In due course shall I hear,' I said, and set foot on the path that my own feet had worn.

As I approached the dark and silent little house crouching amongst the grey out-croppings of limestone I was greeted by the anxious bleat of my goat, Suzanne – the nimble one – who needed milking very urgently, and urgently did I milk her for the splendid white wine of drink she gave me. And, as I milked, night came down, not in darkness, but rather in a lessening of light: an infinitely still half-light, self-evolved, and unrelated to sun or star: a toneless half-light that brought home to one the desolation, the remoteness, the nothingness of immobility – the underlying immobility that is the final and eternal mood. In that still and toneless gloaming I could imagine the world already wheeling dead in dead space but for the occasional little sighing draw of air over far reaches of heather – a sound woefully sad, yet comforting.

CHAPTER IV

It was a hot, still forenoon. I was seated on an old deckchair outside the door of my cottage that nestles on the sunny side of Cairn Rua, below the wood of dark pine and above the shining water of Loch Ruighi. With elbow on one knee, writing-pad on the other, and pipe in mouth, I was wrestling with words and ideas, and losing grip every other sentence. For I was feeling lazy that morning, and was ready to be distracted by little things. My *Early Rose* potato-shaws, lengthening and leaning in the sun, had already cast their blossoms, and I considered at needless length the luxury of new potatoes, salt, and goat's milk for dinner. Also the bell-heather was out in purple splashes all over the lower hillside, and my bees filled the air with the ecstatic hum of the treasure-laden. I cast a contemplative eye on one big double-walled hive where the hum was uproarious, and where a little cluster of bees had commenced to gather below the shelter-porch.

'You will be swarming today, little fellows,' I addressed them, 'and here am I waiting on you.'

What with the heat and the hum and my own innate laziness I was almost in a doze, chin on breast and pipe sagging, when I was roused by the blare of an electric horn. The pipe dropped between my knees, and I sat up with a jerk and stared to where the road curved with the shore of Loch Ruighi, a bare quarter of a mile below me. A motor – a grey touring car not quite unfamiliar – was halted at the point where the path reached the road, and people – several people – were alighting from it.

'Thunder and likewise *blitzen*! Has my young woman in white already started her game?'

For amongst the browns and greys of holiday-clothed men I made out the white dress of a woman; and the squat, familiar figure of Davy Thomson, the head keeper, I could not mistake at that distance.

Head thrown forward and arms crossed, I contemplated them as they came up the path that wound in the heather amongst the outcroppings of lichened limestone. There were Leng the big man, Murray the lean one, Davy Thomson, sturdy and old, and my lady in white. The path was steep and they came slowly, and I had time to consider. Usually have I been lucky in having time given me to weigh things, and that luck has earned me a reputation for coolness in rough places. Also, like most lonely men, I had a habit of speaking to myself.

'What they come for I can only guess at, but it would be a good guess. Until I know what they know and what the woman has told them, I must play an elusive game in the dark. Let us be calm at all costs, and humorous if we can, and avoid quarrelling over trifles with one's poor fellow, who is bound on his own wheel of pride and privilege. Better we cannot do.'

When they came to the green level before the house – the green level cropped short by Suzanne, where thyme grows and a little yellow-flowered trefoil – I rose to my feet and waited. Davy, always a courtly old man, led them forward and did the only introducing he thought necessary.

'A fine warm day the day, Mr King,' said he. 'This is Mr Leng, oor new tenant at Reroppe yonder, an' he wad like to be speirin' a few questions.'

Leng nodded shortly, and I bowed with some precision and a small gesture of the hand.

'Who made the world, Davy, and when and why? – all these questions I can answer, and more as well,' I said, and Murray laughed.

I looked them all over with an appraising eye and waited. Leng was a very tall, splendidly-built man, just the least degree gone to flesh: a splendid, handsome, duskily-flushed, infernally proud young giant, and a good man amongst men it could be; what he was amongst women, one might surmise curiously, judging by his moulded lips and heavy round jowl. Murray was a tall man and desperately lean. Davy Thomson was sturdy, bearded, wrinkled, masked with the serving-man's mask, and he supported his strong old legs on my good hazel staff.

My lady was very beautiful and very calm, and her face was masked too. It told me nothing that I wanted to know.

I swung the deckchair forward to her side, and 'Will the lady be seated?' said I. She bowed her dark head slightly, placed a gloved hand on the top bar of the chair, but did not take the seat.

'Is she my enemy, then, that she will not sit?' I wondered to myself.

Leng, who had been eyeing me with some intentness, started bluntly.

'We are looking for two young fellows,' he said, 'and suspect that they were in this vicinity yesterday. We thought you would be able to give us some information.'

He stopped there and looked to me for an answer, and I could not tell whether he expected an avowal of service or a show of embarrassment.

'Well, Mr Leng,' said I, 'and what information could I be giving you?'

'Did you see two young fellows about or on the loch yesterday?'

'Well, now,' said I thoughtfully, 'I might, and, again, I might not. Were they friends of yours, Mr Leng?'

His black bar of brow came down a little and his Southern voice coldened noticeably. He would, of course, hate to be questioned by a rough-looking devil who lived in a 'black' house on a hillside.

'What has that to do with the plain question I asked you?' he asked.

'I would not be calling it a plain question, Mr Leng. Why would you be looking for two young fellows?'

'Not for their good, I assure you,' he said crisply.

'Exactly! How would you expect me to answer your question?'

'Directly and briefly, of course.'

'And if I said I had not seen your two young men, would you suspect me of lying?'

I think he was about to blurt out a warm affirmative, but I stopped him.

'Please don't, Mr Leng. Let me put it another way. You seek two young men – not for their good, I note. If I had not seen them yesterday I could say so, but if I had and they were friends of mine I might, if the occasion demanded, give a similar answer to an angry man looking for them.'

'What is your answer, then?' he asked shrewdly. 'I am an angry man looking for them.'

'Humble though I be, Mr Leng, I dislike answering any question in the dark; want of confidence discourages me. Moreover, the young men may be thirled to the righteous end in this apparent feud, and I would not like to bear witness against righteousness. How am I to know unless I am told? Only a simple hermit, I have not yet succeeded in subduing pride. You will take me into your confidence, or else—'

'Or else what, sir?' he smiled, a little contemptuously.

'Or else you can sit on the hot hob of hell for a thousand years,' I said simply; 'and God forgive me for using such language before a lady!'

I bowed to her, and nearly laughed at the astonishment on her face. Mr Leng was astonished too and outraged as well, but had no time for reaction before his friend Murray saved the situation for the time. A bark of genuine laughter came from him, and he stepped forward to the big man's side.

'Mr King is more or less right, Leng,' he said. 'If you want any information you'll have to be frank and explain why you are an angry man justly.'

Leng's face was flushed, and the anger in his dark eyes was full of menace and a hearty desire for action. 'What's the use in bandying words?' he said to his friend, and there stopped abruptly as if a fresh thought had come to him. He looked at me intently, calculatingly, almost cunningly. 'Ah!' he said, almost to himself, 'perhaps I see your point, Mr King. We will forget your language and try you out another way.' And then he went on very quickly. 'Yesterday we caught two young poachers on the Leonach—'

Here a certain memory led me to interrupt him. 'Were you trying the fish, by any chance, yourself?'

'Of course.'

'You caught no salmon yesterday surely?' I said, an eyebrow lifted.

'We did,' said Murray quickly, 'and a nice twelve-pounder at that.'

'Man alive!' I cried, with enthusiasm, 'that was grand fishing for a hopeless day. Was it on a minnow or an eel-tail?'

'That can wait,' said Leng hurriedly, but I had caught the lean one's smile and the half-shamed grin of Davy Thomson.

Quickly and fairly Leng narrated the previous day's doings, as he had seen them, up to the point where the car had been run away with. There he stopped, and I asked with some show of surprise: 'Do you tell me that two bare-footed wastrels were able to steal and manipulate your car?'

'There is where we should like some elucidation, sir,' he replied. 'The chauffeur insists that the two were fully clothed when they assaulted him. And that points to an accomplice – and one who must be acquainted with Reroppe.'

'And whom would you be suspecting?' I asked interestedly.

'By heavens, sir,' he cried, coming to the crux bluntly, 'we suspect you!'

'I was beginning to suspect the same,' I said sadly. 'And would you tell me now on what you base your suspicions?'

Here I looked evenly at the lady, expecting to read in her face that she had borne witness against me. But she looked at me with equal smoothness, and neither face nor eyes gave any sign. Her face was calm, nonchalant, grave, almost austere, and her eyes were dark and still below the rim of the panama. I was about to turn my eyes back to Leng, when with a natural ease she drew the deckchair a little round and sank into it, joining her white-gloved hands in her lap, and thrusting forward a neat white shoe to focus her eyes thereon. Her action gave me heart of grace, for it was the act of no enemy, but a plain enough intimation that she was still a neutral. Knowing that, I could still play with Leng's suspicions. He was very decided, and did not hesitate to voice them.

'In the first place,' he said, 'your fencing, alone, would make you suspect. I put you a plain question, and, instead of answering, you have been cross-questioning me in your native fashion. But you are not dealing with fools, Mr King.'

'I cannot tell you whether I am not,' I said.

Here Murray, that imperturbable lean man, took a decisive part.

'Let us have a little clarity,' he said. 'There is no use in going into abstract grounds for suspicion. The fact is, Mr King, that we do not know if you were on the Leonach yesterday; we do not know if you were the third and wisest member of a re-doubtable poaching party.'

I gave this man all my attention, for he was no fool, at any rate.

'All the same we have some grounds for suspicion,' he went on. 'I'll give you the facts, and you can give us your opinion if you like. It was too late last night to take any steps to recover the car, and this morning before calling in the police – a difficult business in these wilds – we decided to take a look around.'

'And found your car?' I side-nodded towards the road.

'Yes. That's it down there. We found it where your road joins the road from Reroppe to Bridge of Carr. This road of yours is very seldom used, we noticed, and it has a fine track-retaining dust. Besides the track of the car we also found the track of a motor-cycle with a side-car, and that track we followed back to its halting-place, where your path reaches the road. You will forgive us if we made a few deductions.'

'I will, surely,' I said, 'and I am obliged by your frankness. Tell me, now, did you find anything else worth mentioning?'

'Queer enough, we found our two salmon – the one killed by us, and the one snared by the lads. They had been overlooked in the car at Reroppe, and the poachers seemed to have overlooked them too.'

' 'Tis just the thing that poachers would do,' I said with

sarcasm, and I felt proud of my two young friends. Also I felt a wave of anger against the man Leng, but did not care to show it.

'Well, well!' I said resignedly, 'you are entitled to your deductions. I am suspect indeed, and, being suspect, what faith can you place in me?'

'Do you admit you were the third party, then?' questioned Leng quickly.

'What use would that be to me?' I said. 'But if you will listen I would like to put a few considerations before you.'

'Go on, sir,' said Leng. 'We would condemn no one unheard.'

'You would not, indeed! As I see it, your case against the two young men is for poaching and illegal fishing. The subsequent events are in the nature of a nice little vendetta, and proceeded directly and naturally from, shall we say, your slightly over-vigorous expression of authority? You might be magnanimous enough, Mr Leng, to base your case on illegal fishing?'

'Suppose I do, Mr King?'

'I am sure, then, you would never charge anyone with what you yourself might be charged with.'

'What do you mean?' he asked frowningly. I had touched him.

'I mean, sir, that not even a fishing proprietor is entitled to lift salmon from a pool by means of a long-handled gaff. I don't see why he shouldn't, occasionally – when the fishing is slow – but there it is.'

Well I knew that long-handled gaff and Davy Thomson's expertness in wielding it, and it was clear that neither of the fish caught yesterday had been caught fairly.

'You are admitting, then,' questioned Leng, 'that you saw me, yesterday, killing salmon in that way?'

'I will not admit anything, and will not ask you to admit anything either.'

'You are magnanimous.'

'And would like you to be.'

'You have no right to make that request.'

'Be reasonable, then. You must see how I am placed.'

32

'I do; and, having learned what I wanted to know, will now bid you good day.'

'Consider this before you go, then. Your position is quite untenable.'

'We shall see as to that.'

'It is, you know. You cannot very well prosecute where you yourself are equally in the wrong. As regards the mere poaching, you acted like a man of spirit and hot blood, though rather high-handedly. You man-handled one of them, who resented it in like manner; then you illegally arrested them, took them down that rough river-bed bare-footed, and finally locked them up in your garage. Autocratic work that, Mr Leng! With or without an accomplice they got away in your car, and showed their contempt for your salmon. Strange poachers surely, Mr Leng?'

'Anything else to add, Mr King?'

'Only that you would be well advised to forget that anything happened yesterday. You have recovered your car and your salmon; you punished the lads rather severely, and acquired only that reasonable black-eye in return; and altogether the advantage is yours, whether you deserve it or not. I do not think you do, but that will not worry you. And another thing, Mr Leng – you pay me a compliment in thinking that these lads are friends of mine, and I regret that, in return, I am unable to give you any information. That is final, and you will just have to do what you please about it.'

I looked him straight in the eye, and waited for what he might have to say. And somehow at that moment he had no words ready to his tongue.

And then, before he could summon up a fitting speech, my big double-walled hive swarmed in fury and delight.

CHAPTER V

That sudden swarming banished from my mind the little fog of anger engendered by our petty human squabbles. No lover of bees can be obsessed by any alien passion during the excitement of a swarm. We were within twenty yards of the hive, and the excited bees were in the air all around us, wheeling, whirling, and roaring their joyous swarming song. A stream of them was pouring from the wide, low doorway of the hive and taking the air in dizzy, wide sweeps. The sky above us was a network of darting, curving, zigzag lines, wholly dazzling to the eyes, and queerly exciting to the blood.

'Don't let us be doing anything foolish, Mr Leng,' said I; 'and you'll excuse me for a little while.'

And for the moment I forgot all about my visitors and their errand. My task, and an urgent one, was to induce the bees to cluster on some convenient bush before they had yet made up their minds to set off for the ancient honey-holes in the ruined stronghold on the Wolf's Island. I rushed indoors and forth again, carrying a pail of water and my garden syringe. With the latter I sprayed vigorously here and there amongst the darting bees, creating the illusion of a shower – and there is nothing so distasteful to swarming bees. Their instinct at once tells them to cluster protectingly around their beloved queen on the first suitable bush. Man's reason, though more imperfect than the instinct of the insect, is more elastic, and is for ever winning partial victory. Presently I noticed a vortex in the flying swarm, and located its centre above an old lichened gooseberry-bush at the back of the mother-hive and just within the gate of my garden patch. Jetting a final spray into the air, I dropped the syringe, again hurried indoors, and this time brought forth a white tablecloth. Already, on the main stem of the bush, a cluster was forming and growing every instant, and I carefully arranged the cloth on the gnarled and thorny arms, so that, while giving the bees room to cluster, it also shaded them from the fierce sun-glare. Having done this to my satisfaction, I wiped a heated brow and looked around me.

A swarm is marvellously exciting to every healthy and unavaricious lover of bees. The fever in the adventuring insects, the high spirit that is hurtling them forth to found a new state, infects a man. For five minutes or more I had been hopping round and into my little garden, trampling the cabbages, getting tangled in the potato-shaws, leaping over the berry-bushes – and not in any dull silence either. Probably I swore with

34

fluent joviality, shouted picturesque encouragement, gave forth various cries, yells, or raucous bellows, and even ventured a stave or two of song:

There was an old woman tossed up in a blanket seventy times as high as the moon.
Where she was going I couldn't but ax her, for in her hand she carried a broom.
    'Old 'oman, old 'oman, old 'oman,' says I,
    'Where are you going up so high?'
    'To sweep the cobwebs offn the sky,
    An' I will be with ye to-morrow by-'m'by.'

Or perhaps it was:

Brian O'Linn and his wife and wife's mother, they all went over the bridge together.
The bridge fell down and the mother fell in. 'She'll be found at the bottom,' says Brian O'Linn.

Or maybe it was:

Oh! I do love a lady – she's fairer than they say.
Her beauty has a secret that haunts me night and day.
Her face is neither fair nor white, nor brooding is her eye,
But I must love that lady until the day I die.

And so my brow needed wiping. And as I wiped it I looked towards the spot where my visitors had been. They were not there any longer. But almost within arm's-reach, in the gateway of the garden, stood my lady in white, and over her shoulder peeped Davy Thomson. She, too, looked as if her brow needed wiping. Her dark eyes were alive – no longer half-weary below heavy lashes – there was the faintest colour in her cheeks – faint, but more suggestive than a million flushes – and her lips were a little parted. She was very beautiful.

I craned a head to look over the dry-stone wall towards the road, and the lady spoke. 'My friends are gone,' she explained. 'They have some business at Barnagh station, and I sent them

35

away. They will call for me on their return. I am glad I did not miss this, and would have liked to sing that last song with you. You are not a very good singer, Mr King.'

'No, ma'am,' said I agreeably, 'but I have grand tunes in my head.'

For the first time I liked this lady; for the first time my indifference – or disinterested appreciation – gave way to a distinct liking. 'Do you know the ways of bees, my lady?' I asked her.

'Only that they sting as well as sing,' she replied. 'What are they doing under that cloth?'

'Myself I do not know. The authorities say that they are marshalling forces and awaiting the report of scouts sent out to reconnoitre a new home. 'Tis a guess by the authorities, I suspect.'

'Are they leaving here, then?'

'Not if I can help it. I have a snug home of my own for them.'

Here Davy Thomson spoke up. 'I maun help you hive the wee beasties, Mr King,' he said. 'Miss de Burc micht like to ken fu it's done. Rin ye in for the auld rusky, an' I'll gi'e the clout a sprinkle or two meantime.'

'Thank you, Davy,' I said – 'You must not be afraid of a sting, Miss de Burc. Swarming bees rarely sting. If one gets into your hair, the unchivalrous rogue might not respect its beauty, but you are reasonably safe while wearing that panama.'

'I will take the risk,' she said, ignoring the half-compliment.

With Davy's deft assistance I persuaded the swarm to move up into a straw skep – or rusky, as he called it – placed on the arms of the bush above the cluster. And from that we gingerly moved it to the nearby floorboard of the frame hive that was to be the home of the new colony. During the different operations the lady moved about interestedly and without fear – a fair test for any lady – and, no bee venturing the insidious net of her hair, I had no opportunity of feeling its soft texture, or of admiring at very close quarters the column of her neck and the colour of it.

While the work was going on we talked of bees and the little

36

we knew about them, and when the work was done we sat for a little space on the rude bench by my cottage wall in the pleasant warmth of early afternoon, and talked of other things, our eyes wandering across the sun-hazed expanse of loch to the shimmering roll of moors that lifted up and up into the blunt head of Aitnoch Hill.

'Sit ye doon, Davy,' I invited the old man, who had been diffident in resting his sturdy legs in the presence of a lady of caste. 'I am greatly obliged to you for bringing back my hazel staff; I would be sorry to lose it.'

Davy glanced across me at the lady, and there was discomfort in his eye.

'It is all right, Davy,' she said with understanding. 'I caught the criminal all by myself yesterday. We seem to be accomplices after the fact.'

'Fine I kent the staff, Mr King,' said Davy, hiding his surprise, 'an' a gey pity it was that I didna notice it looped on tae yon salmon until we had thae lads grippit.'

'It was only a ploy on our part, Davy,' I said, putting a hand on his knee. 'We were foolish, but we meant no harm, and I promise you it will not happen again.'

'I ken fine ye dinna mak' a practice o' yon, Mr King. Man, I am gey sorry it happened at all, for it will gang further nor this, an' the end o 't will be a visit from the Lady o' Clunas an' a tongue-lashing for baith o's. Mr Leng is a very angry man the day, an' is no' easy persuadit in that mood.'

'He certainly was angry,' said the lady.

'I grant that he has some excuse,' I said. 'All the same, madam, it is angrier still he would be if I had my way, and 'tis twice as angry he would be if your friend, Mr Murray, had let my friend, the Irishman, deal with him yesterday on the Leonach side.'

'I think you are mistaken there,' said my lady quietly. 'You do not know Ted – Mr Leng. He is immensely strong, and very famous as an amateur boxer. Your Irishman – or—'

'Or myself,' said I, noting her pause.

'Yes, or yourself,' she nodded, 'or anyone I know, would be little in his hands.'

I could not say anything to that, but her words reminded

me that this lady, who was not of our camp, deserved grati-
tude, and the show of it, for what she had done – or rather not
done – the previous day.

'Madam,' said I, 'considering that your friends are not mine,
I owe you a good deal, and more besides, for not betraying –
that is the wrong word – for not disclosing to your friends the
doubtful situation you found me in yesterday. For a long time
I mistrusted you, and my discussion with yon bonny man was
rather difficult; but once you seated yourself in my old canvas
chair I knew you were no enemy. Your magnanimity has made
the situation very much easier, and I am indeed grateful. You
were infinitely the best sportsman of the lot of us.'

The little tinge of colour that meant so much was again in
her face. I think that she was pleased.

'You flatter me,' she said. 'I am afraid it was not sportsman-
ship that kept me silent, but a feminine dislike for the whole
episode. In parts it was abominable, and I decided to have no
part in it.'

'Your instinct was right, and that was everything.'

'There is one thing that still puzzles me,' she went on, falling into her favourite attitude, hands joined in her lap, head
leaning a little forward, and eyes focused on a thrust-out shoe-
toe, 'and it is that, as much as your swarm, that made me stay
behind my friends today. I could not, and I cannot even now,
understand why you remained hidden yesterday while your
friends were in difficulties. It is queer how that has puzzled and
disturbed me. I would like to think – I suppose it is for the
sake of my own conscience – that you had some purpose in
view.'

'I had. And I am all the more grateful that, doubting my
spirit, you still remained silent. How shall I explain to you?
My friends of yesterday happen to be unknown to Davy here
or to any of the others. As long as they remained unknown
there was a chance for them. My appearance on the scene
would kill that chance. As long as they remained silent I felt
that I – on the wings, as it were – could get them out of the
scrape. And I did, you know. You see, my lady, I was and am
very anxious that the affair should not become public, for if it
goes as far as the sheriff's court, my two young friends might

suffer in their profession, apart from any legal penalty. That is what moved me and moved me strongly, though it sounds weak in the telling. I cannot put it plainer than that.'

'I think I understand,' she said, after a little pause; and, turning to Davy, 'You and I, Davy, must still fill the rôle of accomplices after the fact.'

'I'll hau'd a still tongue, Miss de Burc,' said Davy, 'if that's what you mean.'

With some curiosity, I noticed in myself a desire to stand well with this lady. Never before had I noticed a desire similar. She sat within a yard of me, and a faint perfume of ozone and something more intangible reached me, and no doubt, stirred something from its dormancy in my tough recesses. I glanced sideways at the clean-cut, still profile, with the eyes half-hooded by heavy black lashes, and I found myself wondering what thoughts moved below that very adequate mask.

We were silent for quite a space, each in some lazy haze of aimless reverie or speculation – a silence without embarrassment, and, to me, oddly companionable. Then my lady roused herself and rose to her feet.

'Is it time to be on the top o' the road, Miss?' said Davy, following suit.

'I think I will stroll along the shore-road and meet my friends,' she proposed.

'My lady,' I said, on my feet also, 'do not be thinking I lack hospitality. It is but poor refreshment my old hovel can offer, and none of it fit for the tender palate of the South, but I offer what I have, all the same.'

'That sounds like a dare,' she laughed; 'but I will not be so rude as to ask for your bill of fare.'

''Tis too early for tea,' I said, 'and not late enough for coffee. Wine I have none, and my whisky is some hefty, while those good men, McVitie & Price, have neglected me this week. Still, I possess a goat Suzanne – a nimble lady – who yields a milk whiter than curd and compounded of heather, honey, juniper, and a small spice of goat. New potatoes there be also, and an honest table-salt. New potatoes boiled in spring water, dipped lightly in salt, and washed down with goat's milk: that dish I offer and none other.'

39

'That dish I have not tasted,' she said, falling into my way of speech. 'I should like to try it.'

' 'Tis a fine wholesome diet,' put in Davy. 'Will I lift a two-three shaws for you, Mr King?'

While Davy lifted the new potatoes the lady and I went to where Suzanne was tethered at the rear of the house – tethered so that she could reach the heather on one side, the short hill herbage on the other, with a juniper bush near by for relish. Suzanne was not a long-pedigreed Nubian lady, nor a Salz-burger, nor yet an Anatolian aristocrat, but a plain Scottish nanny-goat of pre-Pictish origin, dingy white in colour, with down-curving horns, a beard biscuit-tinted, and no manners. She greeted us with a lively bleat, a jaunty sideward dance, and a sort of rearing spar on her hind-legs, head down and horns at the attack.

'Dear me! She looks dangerous,' said the lady doubtfully, coming to an abrupt halt.

'A perfect terror,' I agreed. 'Watch how brave I am.'

I went forward in a fighting crouch, side-stepping craftily, chin tucked in, and, the tin milking-pail advanced as a weapon and a shield, patted the rearing Suzanne on the nose, scratched between her horns, and threw an arm over her back; and in a moment the white lances of milk were hissing in the pail, while the dangerous Suzanne stood sleepily still and flicked an ear against a horn.

The lady's laugh rang out behind us. 'You and your goat!' She came boldly at my shoulder and rubbed gently the broad, grizzled forehead of Suzanne.

It might well be that we made a rather good and homely picture, a scene out of old Greece – or even farther East – in spite of my old homespuns and her fashionably-cut attire. The goat is beyond doubt a classic animal, and like enough, Suzanne's ancestors came out of the East before the Milesians. And, as already said, there was something robe-like in the white dress of the lady. It was a very modern dress too, short in the skirt, and showing a thoroughbred pair of ankles. It was the figure below the dress that gave it the classic note: the length of limb faintly defined, the flattish body, the high-set bust gently swelling, the neck set well back on splendid shoulders, the slightly forward poise of head, and the whole lazy, lissome, relaxed length of her – and the quiet. When I have said all there is to say I must come back to the serene yet sombre quietude of that lady. She was as quiet as fate, and as unafraid of what fate had brought her as any goddess in old Greece.

When we returned to the front of the cottage Davy was washing the pink *Early Rose* potatoes.

'Now, my lady,' I said, 'I will invite you into my parlour, and you must admire the splendours of this my castle. It is an ancient house, not one day younger than the ruins of the Wolf's stronghold out there in the water, and it has outlasted that stronghold as a habitation for man a matter of three hundred years. It is but thirty feet in length and half that in width, and the walls of unhewn, mortarless grey stone slope a little inwards. It squats crouchingly on the breast of the hill, prepared to lean a stubborn shoulder to any wind that blows, and its squash hat of good rye-thatch is pulled well over its eyes, which are small, as you see, and no cleaner than they might be. This porch, now, is a modern contrivance and a pure luxury, but it prevents the strong air of the hills from blowing the peats off the hearth on windy days. Now, my lady, we open this inner door, and I usher you into the guest-chamber and the living-room – and the sleeping-room also, though you notice nothing in the nature of a brass bed or an oaken tester; that humble roll in the corner is a hammock which I sling from this hook to yon one, and wherein I pound my ear for ten hours at a stretch. Do you like my room, madam?'

'It is a Spartan room,' said my lady.

'A room of sybaritic luxury rather, O dweller in palaces! Look well, now! Instead of an earthen floor we have reasonably clean white boards with a skin or two; instead of a hole in the roof we have a chimney of stone and an open hearth of brick; for creepie-stools we have basket-chairs, and cushioned at that; and note you my dresser of blue delft, my white-wood table, my writing-desk below the window, and the swinging-lamp to throw light over my left shoulder, and my shelves of books – Swinburne, and James Stephens, and Neil Munro, and Conrad, and Anatole France, and Shaw, and all the Mike Scanlons besides – even Chesterton and Marx.'

'It is a very splendid room indeed,' admitted my lady. 'One would never be lonely in this room.'

There was an odd note in her voice as she said that – 'One would never be lonely in this room' – a note of longing and some inexpressible regret that somewhere touched a chord in me: a deep, heavy chord that boomed like a drum in high tragedy.

'No,' I agreed subduedly, 'one should not be lonely in this room.' And I said very little more until the white deal was covered with a whiter cloth, and plates, cutlery, and glasses were arranged. By that time the potatoes were boiled, strained, and poured into an old blue ashet in mid-table, where they steamed to the black rafters.

'Draw in about, my people,' I invited, 'and do ye as I do. I was a barbarian with this rare vegetable until painfully instructed by an Irishman, who held that it was unspeakable to touch the outside of a potato with the fingers. You take it so on your fork and peel it with serious method. This being a new one, and Davy having scrubbed away cuticle, epidermis, and true skin, only a touch here and there is necessary by way of ritual. Then we cut it in two or in four according to one's orificial ability, and we dip it gently in honest common salt – and so goodbye – and, with a hand towards our white wine, we will down with popes, priests, presbyterians, princes, potentates, and powers who know not this dish. How like ye it?'

The lady laughed a rippling low laugh. 'I was watching you with open mouth,' she said. 'Now I shall try.'

She enjoyed that meal, and, of course, Davy did. Not being bred with any country prejudices she had no objection to goat, and the slightly bitter tang of the milk pleased her. And, indeed, the delicate flavour of new potatoes, combined with the savour of salt and the tang of goat's milk, is well worth the appreciation of unspoiled palates. It was a new and not-to-be-forgotten flavour for this lady from the South.

'I am glad I accepted your entertainment, Mr King,' she thanked me.

42

'I am glad too, madam. It is welcome you always will be to the best I have.'

She smiled a little, and I went on admiring the deft and graceful fingers of her manipulating a hot potato.

We had but finished our repast when the blare of a klaxon-horn came up to us from the road, and our party came to an end. I saw my guests as far as the car, where the lady gave me her hand frankly, but it was a gloved hand, and all I could tell was that it grasped my rough one with firmness.

Murray vacated his seat by Leng, who was driving, and the lady glided into it gracefully.

'Did you enjoy the swarm?' Murray asked her. 'Where are your stings?'

'No stings, slings, or arrows today,' she said over her shoulder. 'Mr King entertained us as his name implies.'

Murray gave me a cordial hand. 'I am very glad to have met you,' he said, and preceded Davy into the back seat.

Leng said no word at all. His face was set into a high indifference, but all the same he looked at me with a calculating eye. He gave me a short nod, touched the accelerator, and I was left alone in the dusty road, shoulders hunched, hands in pockets, and eyes downcast and contemplative.

'That lady,' I mused, 'is a beautiful lady, and a quiet one. She did not say much on this day of much talk, and what she said was said simply and in no foreign tongue. I talked a good deal myself, and twice she laughed. Her voice is a deep voice and a deliberate one, and it has the little vibrant tremor of voices that are used effectively and sparingly. I would like to hear her speak often, but I would not like her often to say: "One would never be lonely in this room." There was a bleak, toneless something in the way she said that. Ah! Well, well!'

CHAPTER VI

I did not at once go back to my cottage – to the room in which one should not be lonely. Instead, I looked across the loch to where the slated crofter's house of the MacGillivrays stood, a hundred yards or so above a clump of willows at the water's edge. One side of Loch Ruighi was my domain, the other and all the moors back to the crown of Aitnoch Hill was tenanted by Hamish MacGillivray, who tilled a few stony acres and grazed his flocks on all the hills. The MacGillivrays were good neighbours, and I might say my only ones, for, after theirs, the nearest house was Reroppe Lodge, four miles across the heather.

'I will pull over and have a news with Archie,' I said, moving down to the home-made berthage where my little cockle-shell was moored.

Mark that Hamish was the crofter, a married man without children, and that Archie was his brother. Archie was a free man who acknowledged no ties, a fisher of note, a deadly shot, learned in all the lore of the hills and the clans: a man of strange culture, and infinitely worth knowing. He had taught me all I knew about rod-fishing and the killing of fish. In all airts of the wind he knew where on the loch the best brown trout would rise to the fly, and even on days when no fish would rise he had lures of his own that never failed us. He took his due toll from the hill too – grouse and white hares – but he was no conscienceless poacher: he used neither gun nor snare during August and September, and hen-grouse he never touched. Davy Thomson could never complain that there were too many cocks on the moor in spring, and he did not inquire too closely into Archie's activities. Archie owned a boat which he called the *Nancy* – a fifteen-foot ship's gig that moved crabwise about the loch because of a kink in her keel, but so seaworthy that she was held to be unswampable. Any visiting angler of whom Archie approved – and he was a keen judge of anglers and men – was welcome to the *Nancy*, but all Philistines were either denied the boat or had to pay a stiff hire for her.

I lazily pulled across the mile of flat water and moored my skiff to the stern of the *Nancy*, where she lay below the willows in a dock similar to my own. Stepping ashore, I was met by a black half-collie, half-retriever, who showed his teeth in a grin of welcome, wagged his tail while I pulled his silky ears, and then, with a definite exercise of reason, led me to where Archie was stacking peats on the edge of the moor, with the *canna-*

44

bawn blowing all around him in the damp hollows – the white canna, the bog-cotton, the mystic flower of the old Gaelic singers.

' 'Tis fine weather that does be in it, Archie MacGillivray,' I greeted him, 'and God bless the work!'

' 'Tis yourself, Mr King,' he said in his drawling Highland accent, straightening himself slowly, a black divot in either hand. 'A fine day whatever, and grand for the peats.'

He was a long, lean man, with two or three bends in him like a gnarled birch tree, attired in the patched saffron-brown of the Gael, with deep-set blue eyes very much alive, and a great mat of soft nut-brown beard hiding most of his face. One could learn nothing and everything from Archie's face.

'I have footed turf as far away as Kerry,' I told him, 'where the art is properly known, and I will now show you how it should be done.'

So I bent my back by his, and together we built little pyramids of peats for the wind to dry; and as we worked we talked. I told him all the previous day's ploy on the Leonach, and we laughed together at the right places.

'You are a terrible man, Mr King,' he said at the end, 'and them two young gaugers are near as bad as yourself. It would be a bad job for them if the day's work was brought home.'

'And a bad job for Mr Leng too, Archie.'

' 'Tis a bad job for him as it is, only maybe he is not sorry. He is a man, I am thinking, would not be sorry for anything, and he is no feart either.'

'Have you met him, then?'

'He was over the hill the beginning of the week with Davy Thomson. He wanted to hire the *Nancy* for a month or two for the trout-fishing. I was no' that keen on letting the bit boat for that long, but he persuaded me, and he had to pay dear for overbearing me. Ay! he is an overbearing man, and I couldn't be bothered countering him in a small thing like the hire of the boatie. There was another man with him, who would be your Mr Murray, and I am thinking he had his pairts.'

'And did you see the lady?' I asked him with some curiosity, for his opinion would be worth having.

'There was no young lady with them,' he replied. 'She will

45

be a young woman, you tell me, and bonny too, and she will be doing any harm that comes of yesterday's ploy.'

'I think she can be trusted not to,' I demurred. 'But, nevertheless, she is one that does harm, despite her, and you will tell me the same thing after you have seen her.'

'Maybe I am not understanding you, Mr King,' said Archie quaintly; 'but I will be looking at her with my two eyes whatever. She will do no harm to a middling old fellow like me, and you are no' that young yourself either. Ay! but you are young enough, Mr King – you are young enough, I am saying.'

'But tough, Archie lad,' was all I said; but just then I felt neither tough nor old.

When the last of the peats were stacked we went down to the house where Hamish and Helen, his wife, were having their evening porridge in the peat-perfumed, earthen-floored kitchen, and I was welcomed hospitably. A great plate of perfectly made, home-grown, home-ground oatmeal porridge, with a beechen piggin of milk fresh from the byre, did I get rid of, and then we men had each a brace of hot, salt-buttered scones and a mug of scalding-hot, bitterly-strong tea. Before I left, Helen, aware of my liking for a stale scone, made up for me a parcel in a white napkin.

And then in the still gloaming I crossed over to my own house – and to the room in which one would not be lonely – and as I dipped oars in the dim-shining water I kept time to an old song I knew:

If I did own the silver moon as well as golden sun,
With Jupiter and Saturn, and planets one by one,
And Sirius, that great dog-star, and mighty belt Orion,
I'd long for still some wee small sun that never yet did shine.

And I was not lonely.

CHAPTER VII

This is the letter I received through the post two days after Mr Leng's inquisitorial visit:

> SIR, – In view of recent circumstances I am compelled to warn you to keep off the property I have rented at Reroppe. If you are found trespassing thereon I shall have to take what steps may be necessary to protect myself. I may state that I have informed Lady Clunas' factor that I have found it necessary to give you the above warning. – Yours,
>
> EDWARD LENG.

'Brief and to the point, Edward,' I mused, 'and yet I am inclined to think that you took a longish time to produce that epistle. You would have liked to say more, but you have said enough. You have virtually proclaimed that our little poaching episode is closed, but that you hope for an early opportunity to jolly well punch my head. We shall be seeing. By heck! If Lady Mary Clunas gets wind of this correspondence she will be up here on a visit of discipline, a thing displeasing to any free man. Now I must write to the ruffians, Quinn and Munro, to keep away from Loch Ruighi for the rest of this season, lest they drown or be drowned by Mr Leng – Edward Leng – Ted, as my lady called him. Ted indeed! I wonder if the good man was displeased with the lady for breaking new potatoes with me – and I wonder how that lady would take his displeasure.'

It will be seen that already I was musing on the relations that might exist between these two.

Lady Clunas did get word of Leng's correspondence, and that very soon. Probably the letter to her factor was in her hands even as I mused over mine, and its perusal bore fruit with characteristic promptitude. That very afternoon as, veiled and gloved, I was inserting additional brood frames in the new hive, the not-often-heard purr of a motor-car came up to me from the shore road. Intent on the rather delicate task that engaged me I did not lift my head to look until the purr slowed down and ceased directly below, and, before I looked, I half expected to see a grey touring car and a lady in white amongst tweed-clad men.

But this car was black, and the lady that alighted from it was also in black, and unaccompanied.

'God be merciful!' I cried; 'it is Lady Mary on the war-path.' Hastily I covered the brood-box, doffed veil and gloves, and went down the path to meet my landlady and what was coming to me.

Lady Clunas was a young war-widow, left with two small sons and great wealth in money and lands. Holding this wealth in trust for these sons, she was quite needlessly economical, and instead of a Rolls-Royce or such she owned no more than a Ford runabout – what the Americans call a 'flivver' – which she jockeyed over the hill roads of her wide estates with great skill and utter recklessness. She was a young woman of immense energy, and with little regard for what are called conventions where they concerned herself; therefore she thought little of coming alone across twenty miles of hills to visit and if necessary demolish me. In truth I liked her very well, and admired her for the real kindliness that her brusqueness could not hide. Also I was not in the least afraid of her, and had great difficulty in hiding the fact, which is why I went down to meet her, pulling a long face.

'Good day, Lady Mary,' I greeted her from a distance. 'You are not a bit welcome this time.'

'I know that,' she cried back, 'but I am coming all the same.'

She gave me her hand very frankly, a small strong hand with a hard palm – and a friendly hand too, as well I knew. We went up the path together. She was not tall, nor, as the mother of two sons, was she exactly sylph-like, but she was a bonny young woman nevertheless: middle-sized, well-shouldered, straight-backed, snugly-built, with reddish, lovely hair, a skin still lovelier, and eyes deeply blue and steady. She was trimly attired in black, a colour that suited her, and she carried herself trigly on neat black brogues.

'I will not talk to you, Tom King,' she said, 'until I have

48

climbed this hill and have some breath to waste. Wasted it will be, too.'

'It will not, dear lady,' I denied stoutly. 'The breath you gently and with art expel through your vocal cords always gives me delight, encouragement, and good advice.'

'Bah!' said Lady Mary.

'Surely,' I agreed. 'That was not a neat way of complimenting the beauty of your voice and the wisdom of your words.'

She shrugged her shoulders, but probably she was not displeased.

'Ma'am,' said I, when we reached the green level before the door, 'here's the block on which I hack sticks for firewood, and yonder is my little axe that never told a lie. I point them out now lest I be afraid to do so later on. I pray you, when the time comes, remove my head with dispatch, for it is an operation of some pain if dallied over.'

'You will sit there on the headsman's block,' she ordered, 'and I will sit here in this canvas chair.'

'Ladies like that chair,' I could not help saying, and she cocked a speculative eye at me.

'I have no objections to your smoking if you want to,' she began, arranging her skirts deftly. 'I am not really angry with you, Tom; I do not even blame you, seeing what and who you are, but there is here a matter that must be cleared up this day.'

'Thunder! Lady Mary,' I protested. 'You are the directest young woman as ever was. That is no way to approach a subject. We have not yet said a word about the weather or the crops, the forward state of the grouse or the poorness of the fishing.'

'We will talk of the fishing, then,' said Lady Mary readily.

'That was a bad break,' I said ruefully. 'Carry on!'

She opened a black baglet she carried – a silken affair with an amber hoop – and brought forth an envelope. She leant back in the canvas chair and crossed a pair of neat silken ankles – economy or none, she insisted on gauze-fine silk stockings – and, cat-like, made herself comfortable. She was going to have a good, righteous time, and I dissembled a smile.

'Listen to this letter,' she began. 'It is from Edward Leng, our new tenant at Reroppe, to my factor, Bill Mavor.'

'I shall certainly knock Bill's head off,' I put in.

She took no notice of that remark, but began reading:

'DEAR SIR—'

'He called me plain sir,' I interrupted.

'DEAR SIR, – Having reason to suspect Mr Thomas King, of Loch Ruighi Cottage, of poaching on the Leonach and of even more outrageous practices, I have warned him not to trespass on the policies rented by me from Lady Clunas. Whilst not entering into details, I think it my duty to inform you of the action I have been compelled to take, so that, if you think it necessary, a watch may be kept on Mr King as regards the other areas of the Clunas estates.

'That is all,' said Lady Mary, looking inquiringly at me over the top of the letter. 'Will you kindly tell me what it is all about?'

I was filling my pipe industriously. 'It is enough,' I said. 'It is enough, surely, and twice as more. He is an admirable, brief man is Mr Edward Leng – sometimes called Ted.'

'Who calls him Ted?' she asked quickly, her gaze sharpening.

'My lady in white calls him Ted,' I replied simply.

'*Your* lady in white!' she exclaimed. Her look was very intent indeed, and there was at the same time a widening of the eyes that is caused by surprise, or perplexity, or a little sudden fear – but of course it could not be fear.

Again she looked at the letter, and I knew the words her eyes sought. I smiled, and she caught me, and in turn she also smiled, but not very cheerfully.

'You are a wily old fox, Tom,' she said, 'but for the present we will ignore red herrings.'

'You wrong me there. You said, I think, that that libellous letter was addressed to your factor.'

'Meaning, of course, that he should not have shown it to me.'

'Just that,' I agreed.

'Bill Mavor occasionally surprises me. I happened to be in

the estate office this forenoon when this letter was delivered, and Bill Mavor, that sedate man, roared with laughter as he read it – and kept on roaring – just as you are doing now.'

'Forgive me, Lady Mary. Your words made me see old Bill with his head over the back of the chair.'

'That is exactly where his head was. "You'll have to deal with this yourself," he told me. "If I go up there Tom King will merely make fun of the whole affair, and I won't be able to do anything but laugh." There's a nice man for a factor! I don't know, at present, what is the outrageous thing you have done to my tenant, but really, Tom, you are making the smooth running of this part of the estate an impossibility. You can do what you like with Bill Mavor, Davy Thomson, Archie MacGillivray, and the rest.'

'But not with Lady Mary Clunas,' I cried. 'Alas! not with Lady Mary Clunas.'

She had always the bonny red rose in her cheeks, but at my words I thought that a richer colour flushed the rose. 'I should hope not,' she said, 'though I think you have never tried.' And she went on quickly, 'You must understand, Tom, that no man, however we like him, can be allowed to interfere with the smooth running of the Clunas estates. If things go on as this letter would imply, we shall ultimately be unable to let the Reroppe shootings.'

'That is a consideration I did not weigh, my lady,' I said carelessly.

'But you must,' she said persuasively, but not in the least domineeringly. 'I speak not for myself but for my sons, Alistair and Ian, whose trustee I am.'

'Your two boys will have immensely more than is good for them. It would be doing them a good turn to despoil you of some of the ill-gotten Clunas wealth. Any reason why I should not try, Lady Mary?'

'You are being perverse now,' she said tartly. 'There *are* steps I could take, you know.'

'For example, you could eject me from Loch Ruighi here. As your tenant I am at your mercy. Would you like me to go?'

She gave me a sudden flashing glance. 'Sometimes I would,'

she said quickly, and her glance, after holding mine for a moment, sought the ground.

'Say the word and I bundle and go.'

'I will not,' she said firmly. 'You were my husband's best friend.'

That was the truth. Alistair Baron Clunas and myself had seen life together in many strange places, and strange life in many places that were not strange. Since his rather foolhardy death by a sniper's bullet at Delville Wood I had made only one friend I held as dear, and that was Neil Quinn, the cynical and matter-of-fact Irishman. Nevertheless, it was not a flattering position to retain Lady Mary's consideration, to be able carelessly to override her wishes, because I had been her husband's best friend. Therefore I said, with assumed resignation, 'Well, go I must, I suppose.'

She flushed hotly, uncrossed her ankles, and sat up. 'You are a brute, Tom,' she cried, 'and most unfair. You are well aware that I am your friend — if you will have it so — apart from any friendship of the past. If I must say it, your presence — just within the horizon, as it were — gives me confidence in many perplexing places.'

'I somehow wanted to hear you say that, Lady Mary,' I said, 'for I do be liking you myself.'

But I felt uncomfortable at this creeping-in of sentiment, and I went on quickly, 'Oh! but you are the wily one, and you are going to have your own way as usual. Listen you now, and I will tell you what induced Mr Leng to do as he has done.' And briefly I narrated the events of the previous days, making it clear to her that the whole adventure was a mere frolic on our side, inconsiderate of course, but not in the least malicious.

She listened attentively, put one or two shrewd questions, and at the end began, 'If that be all—'

'That is all, I assure you, Lady Mary. Mr Leng has merely an ill-concealed suspicion that I am the man behind the scenes, and is anxious to punish me as I deserve. As a matter of fact I atoned for my offence by saving your valuable tenant and your precious estate a nasty jar, for you know that he acted quite outside his legal rights, to say nothing of his moral ones.'

'You have taken a weight off my mind,' she said, and added,

'though I must discount your solicitude for my precious estate. I shall speak to Mr Leng this very day.'

'I pray you to be prudent. I know of old the temper that goes with that sanguine hair of yours, and your Mr Leng has a temper too.'

'Oh! I know Edward Leng. You may not be aware that we are distantly related.'

'Indeed! It was distant enough, I hope, to make him pay an exorbitant rent for Reroppe.'

'Yes. I am quite aware that you think me a bargain-driver. But just a moment, Tom King. There are still a few things to clear up. For instance, who are your two young friends, and who is this lady that addresses Mr Leng as Ted?'

'My two young friends do not move in your circle, proud aristocrat, and more's the pity for your circle! Let them stay safe and unknown. But I will tell you about the lady. Yesterday – no, the day before – I had a visit of inquisition from Leng, and with him were a tall man named Murray, and—'

'That would be Norman Murray, the famous traveller and mountain-climber.'

'So! He looked and acted a man of parts. Can you also tell me who the lady in white was? She was in the company too.'

'What was she like – overfed and outspent?'

'Not on your life, madam. I wish I could tell you in fitting words. She was Helen, or Cleopatra, or Deirdre in the flesh, this day of our Lord. A tall young woman she was, slim yet substantial, with black hair and little colour, a neck like live marble, and a face as quiet as the angel Gabriel's – a sombre, quiet face, knowing the hopelessness of humanity. Davy Thomson called her Miss de Burc.'

'Agnes de Burc!' exclaimed Lady Mary sharply.

'Not a bit lamb-like, I assure you.'

'Agnes de Burc, all the same,' Lady Mary frowned. 'Yes! she is very beautiful, but what is *she* doing up here with Edward Leng?'

'Note you, my lady, that she called him Ted. That might denote a certain intimacy, or even affection. Spoil not my young dreams: call it friendship if you will, but not affection.'

'Silly! she is his wife's niece.'

'Oh, you certainly know all about them. The wife will be at Reroppe too, I suppose – you mentioned an overfed and out-spent dame.'

'I meant his aunt,' Lady Mary laughed shortly. 'Edward Leng and his wife have lived apart these five years and more. She will not divorce him, though, it is said, she might, and she will not give him a chance to divorce her, though, it is said, he wants to.'

I said nothing for a space, but a queer jumble of speculations came into my mind. Lady Mary was silent too, her small black brogue tapping the grass.

'Quite a situation,' I said at last. 'He struck me as a man not easy to live with.'

'It should not be an easy situation for the niece,' said Lady Mary coldly, rising from the canvas chair. 'I am going round to see him now.'

'Must you? He is a stubborn man. I am the guilty party, and I would not like you treated contumeliously. If you wish, I will go and assure Mr Leng that his rights shall be respected by me and my friends.'

'You have a poor opinion of me, to be sure.'

'How in glory do you make that out?' I cried, genuinely surprised.

'You think, of course, that I came up here for the sake of my estate.'

I had nothing to say to that, for it was exactly what I did think.

'You would never entertain the idea that I was also thinking a little of your interests.' She was sarcastic then, but now she went on, and there was a note of warm sincerity in her voice, 'I would never tolerate any tenant of mine ordering you off the Clunas estates'; and with a little hurt irony she added, 'you were my husband's best friend.'

I threw up my hands. 'Don't shoot any more, lady. I am already full of lead and a moral corpse. This has been a regular field-day with you.'

I felt oddly uncomfortable, and my words were frivolous lest they be sentimental. Lady Clunas had shown me a new side of her character, and I had not yet time to focus it. It seemed to affect me rather closely. 'Will you not have something before you go?' I invited her. 'I have a China tea of some flavour, and Helen MacGillivray's scones are good scones. I should have told you that I am an entertainer of note.'

'Indeed! What further disclosures have you to make?'

'None. You ask Miss de Burc. Shall I put on the kettle?'

She answered absent-mindedly, as if her thoughts were busy about something else, 'No, thanks. I will get some tea at Reroppe.'

Yet I felt that very little pressing would have made her stay. I did not press her.

We went down the hill together.

'Come over to Clunas soon,' she invited, 'or my boys will forget you.'

'I will, surely. It is time I took those scamps in hand. Meantime I will be thinking a lot of you and your goodness to me.'

'I like to be well thought of — by you,' she said, and slid into the driving-seat of her flivver.

I jerked the driving-handle, and watched her disappear in a pother of dust. My bad habit of musing aloud asserted itself. 'You came all the long road from Clunas,' I said, 'not to reprimand me, but to protect. You are a strange young woman this day, and not understood by me. Now you are going round to Mr Leng to instruct him in my prerogatives, and I did not tell you that I would hate to hold privileged position with him from behind your skirts. That would never do at all, my dear, and this very day I shall have to go round to Reroppe and tell him so in the language that is required. I will so, by heck!'

CHAPTER VIII

Later that afternoon I went round to Reroppe, all the way round by the king's highway, like a dutiful subject of my liege-lord, Leng. As I went in the dust of the road or on its heathery margin I considered the man I was going to see — that is, when I could get my mind away from the bonny hills all about me and the far-away blue ramparts of the Grampians.

'Anyway,' I reasoned, 'let us not think too hardly of him. He is a man bound by his own temper and his acquired prejudices, and maybe a kernel of likeableness is to be found in him for the trying. And, moreover, any dislike we bear him, or any rancour, only lowers us to his level. Let us be serene, then, in God's name, and find out if he has any serenity in him. And besides, a certain lady, who is no ordinary woman as I think, seems to like him and is perhaps liked by him – and it may be that she can rule him for his own sake and hers. We will be calm, then, if we can, and probe the cause of like and dislike.'

So that was settled, even though a certain modicum of casuistry had to be employed.

On the head of the long slope of Ard-na-Sidhe I sat on a tuft of heather and smoked a pipe. Northwards and far down the slope was the grey lodge of Reroppe within its belt of pines, and far beyond was the wide stretch of dark woodlands and the narrow northern sea. Behind me was Loch Ruighi wimpling in the afternoon breeze, and beyond it a very welter of round brown hills rolling away and away to the high blue walls of the Grampians – my own hills, all brown and quiet in the slowly-waning day, except where here and there in the nearer hollows the bell-heather spread its ruddy purple splashes.

I admired all that splendid view greatly and at length; and then, having finished my pipe, I went lazy-striding down the hill. There was no hurry. I wanted to give Lady Mary time to take her tea and be gone. But when I got round to the gravelled front of Reroppe there was the lady's battered flivver slouching vagabondly at the front door. I hesitated and for a moment wondered what to do.

'Ah, well!' I said then, 'great courage on my part is here indicated.'

So I went forward and knocked with false boldness, and in due time Elspet Thomson, the housekeeper, opened to me. 'Good evening, Mr King,' said she. 'Is it Davy you'll be wanting?'

'Good evening to you, Elspet, my dear,' I gave back. 'It is not your scoundrelly husband I am wanting. I am a respectable man for once, and seek word with Mr Edward Leng, who owns us all. Is that gentleman inside?'

'He is, then. Come awa' ben, and I'll be getting him for you.'

She put me into the gun-room on the left of the flagged hall, and shut the door carefully on me. The gun-room was a lime-washed apartment, with a stone floor covered with fibre matting, the usual well-filled gun presses and cartridge cabinets, the rests for fishing-tackle, a wide deal table, a few cane chairs, and the ordinary sporting prints. Above the fireplace on the white surface of the wall was a first-class drawing in carbon of grouse driven down-wind, and I was trying to diagnose the remarkable portrayal of speed and air when the door opened to admit Leng.

He was dressed for dinner, and the black and white suited him. He was without doubt a handsome man, with splendidly moulded shoulders and slightly dusky, resolute, rather saturnine face. There was now no scowl on his brow, no ridged jaw muscles, no high and furious colour. Instead, he was very calm, and even smiling a little, as he walked across the floor and carelessly threw a leg over a corner of the table. 'Good evening, Mr King,' he said pleasantly. 'I am glad you have come over to Reroppe.'

'Thank you,' I said; and went on without any preface. 'I have come about that warning letter you sent me, Mr Leng.'

'Yes! I wanted to see you about that,' he said composedly. 'I fear I wrote that letter and another rather hastily, but I hope you will admit that appearances were against you the other day?'

'No doubt of that,' I admitted. Leng surprised me with the handsomeness of his admission, but I was not yet to be driven from the pursuit of my object. 'I have not come to cavil at the tone or justice of your letter, Mr Leng,' I went on, 'but to tell you that I accept its warning in fairness to Lady Clunas' interests and your own.'

'I hope you will let me withdraw that letter?' he requested. 'The whole thing happened rather unfortunately; and Lady Clunas, who, as you may know, is here just now, has put the situation in a different light.'

'She could not alter facts – which are stubborn, you know?'

57

'Still, my facts were rather scanty. I know, of course, that you were implicated, but am now aware that there was no malicious intent on your part. Mind you, King, you were indiscreet at the very least, and you did presume a great deal; but, Lady Clunas having explained your status and – shall we say? – eccentricities, I readily admit that my letter was quite unnecessary, and am prepared to withdraw it and make a fair start with you.'

I considered for a space. There were many things I could say, and somehow it was difficult to appreciate Leng's magnanimity. My cynical mind fastened on the fact that he was being very lenient, and that his principal reason for leniency was what he would call my caste position. That surely called for ridicule. 'In truth, King,' he went on in a burst of confidence, 'I have the very devil of a temper, and did go rather far with those two young scoundrels. And let me say that things might have been a good deal worse, and that you probably acted for the best.'

This was really handsome, and I began to appreciate the manly qualities in the man. I could be churlish no longer. 'I had no right on your water, Mr Leng,' I said, 'and behaved without consideration for the feelings of a new tenant at Reroppe. The whole thing was a thoughtless ploy on my part, and since you are agreeable I shall be glad to forget it ever happened.'

'That is settled, then,' he said with satisfaction, and, jumping off his easy perch on the table, he gave me a frank hand and a strong grip. 'Mind you,' he said, laughing, 'I should like to meet that tall young fellow on a fair field with no interruption for five minutes.' He looked at me with a humorous frown. 'Could you manage it?'

Before I could reply a barbarous gong went mad in the hall outside.

'Never mind for the present,' he said. 'We are having an early dinner for Lady Clunas' sake, as we could not let her across the moors hungry. Stay and have pot-luck with us, King. I am sure Lady Clunas will be glad to see our misunderstanding so amicably settled. You have no hermitic scruples, I hope?'

'None at all.'

'Come, then. The ladies will be in the dining-room. Miss de Burc was greatly charmed with your unique entertainment at Loch Ruighi, and will be glad to see you and play hostess.'

His invitation was perfectly frank, and could not be refused. Indeed, I had no particular desire to refuse. There was no longer any reason for resentment or egotism, and I rather suspect that one or two subconscious considerations urged me to accept.

He threw open the dining-room door at the other side of the hall and ushered me in. 'I think you know most of us,' he said at my shoulder. 'Murray you met yesterday. This is my aunt, Mrs Daire.'

I found myself bowing to a plumpish, brightly-clothed woman, who came over and shook my hand warmly; and I minded Lady Mary's description – 'overfed and outspent'. That peculiar adjective 'raddled' might have been added too, but there was, besides, a gaiety – perhaps slightly vulgar – a kindliness slightly over-ready, a sincerity bordering on the risky, about that poor spent old butterfly that I did like. And perhaps I also liked her because – well, because she was a second woman in that household.

Lady Mary, her fine red hair shining in the evening glow coming through the western windows, seemed quite at home, and evidently her talk with Leng had been a diplomatic one. She lifted her eyebrows a little as our glances met, and then smiled somewhat ruefully. 'You might have saved yourself a walk, Tom,' she said.

'Glad to see you over, King,' called Murray from the other side of the table.

'And I am glad too,' said Agnes de Burc, coming forward and giving me her hand, which was cool and firm, I noted. That was all she said; but her smile, though faint and re-strained, seemed to darken her eyes with some genuine warmth of welcome. It was enough.

Neither of the house ladies was in evening dress – out of deference, no doubt, to the black driving costume of Lady Mary. I have no memory for ladies' attire and all I remember is that Mrs Daire wore something very bright, and Agnes de

Burc something low-necked and easy-fitting that showed off her litheness, her white arms, her slender neck. I mind sitting in my place at the table, my eyes on the cloth, and considering that a man like Leng, young, full-blooded, somehow Eastern in fibre, could scarcely help desiring, pursuing such a woman.

Though far from the haunts of the gourmet, Leng did himself and his guests well. I am no faddist in food – simple fare satisfies, coarse fare suffices; but I can fully appreciate a good dinner well equipped and well served; and that dinner was all that could be desired. Besides, there was a brown sherry with the mellow aftertaste, a château claret, a sparkling moselle for the ladies, and a vintage port thick on the palate. To appreciate a dinner like that one should be washed and shorn and in evening dress to suit the whiteness of the napery, the sheen of the silver, the brilliance of the crystal, the gleam in woman's eyes.

When the salmon came to table Murray wanted me to identify it.

'It should in justice be still in the water, whichever fish it is,' admitted Leng readily.

'Hush!' I warned. 'Lady Mary is listening.'

'I am,' she said; 'and that subject is barred.'

So for a time we talked generalities – the fine shooting prospects, estate matters, the poor business outlook, the vagaries of labour. The last subject one had to be wary on in that company. Leng was frankly reactionary in politics; Murray, a colonial imperialist without any considered views on home affairs; Lady Clunas a hereditary Tory. Mrs Daire was a mere parrot; while Agnes de Burc was a body-politic in herself, and gave us no enlightenment.

Mrs Daire, on my right hand, was not to be contented with generalities. No doubt she looked on me as something of a strange animal, and wanted, as it were, to stick a pin in my sawdust. 'I am curious to see your cottage amongst the hills, Mr King,' she said presently.

'You will be welcome at any hour, madam,' I said gallantly.

'Oh, my! Oh, my!' she said coyly. 'You'll be tired of living all alone, of course? Have you lived long in that lonely place?'

'Not long, Mrs Daire, but I intend to live there for a hundred and twenty-five years.'

'Dear me! You must like it, then?'

'It is my only reason for living there.'

'Are you sure of that, Mr King?' she asked slyly, and the old harridan half-twitched an eyebrow towards Lady Clunas.

'That's right, aunt,' put in Leng. 'Cross-examine him thoroughly – I confess, King, that your choice of home strikes me as – unusual.'

'Yet it is the usual sort of home that a majority of the people live in anywhere.'

'Maybe. But that a man like you should bury himself in these wilds does seem unusual.'

'You will admit, though, that a man should do what he likes to do?'

'Though he is probably wrong,' interrupted Murray, 'that is exactly what Leng will admit. He has always done what he liked.'

'I doubt it,' I argued. 'I doubt if any single one of you has kept on doing what he or she would like. Now, I have – and that is a big boast to make. I have made my home here because I like it, and I like it so well that I will let no consideration drive me out of it, except for an occasional winter jaunt. Now, you people think that you are engrossed in business, politics, society, travel, or what not. You extol work, production, progress, hurry, yet you fly from all these things at every opportunity, and seek out these fastnesses that you may be natural for a little while.'

'Life is variety,' argued Murray.

'Faith, it is not!' I disagreed. 'Life does not like variety.'

'You men are always getting tangled in abstruse discussions,' reproved Lady Clunas.

'So we are, my lady,' I agreed; 'but what I wanted to get at was that I have no use for this gospel of work with a little play, and I have a better opinion of you men than to think that you have much use for that gospel either. It is not so much the play that brought you up here – neither the salmon-fishing, nor the grouse-shooting, nor the rock-climbing either, Mr Murray.'

'Why did we come, then?' asked Murray; and he smiled the smile of one that already knows.

'To be your own selves for a little while – to find yourselves – to correct your perspective – to take stock of life – to shed inessentials – to make a fresh start in the business of living – all these things, and more also.'

Murray gave two or three quick little nods of acquiescence; and Leng, who had been turning a fork over and back on the white cloth, spoke half-musingly: 'There is something in all that. It is in places like this that one does make decisions – momentous, fearless, careless of what stupid people think.'

There was something covert in the glance he sent round the table and allowed to rest for a moment on Miss de Burc. She turned her level gaze on me and asked a question: 'You said that a man should not be afraid to do what he would like to do?'

'Nor yet a woman, of course.'

'Do you mean that seriously?'

'Now that you put it like that, I must pare down that didactic statement to the proportions where it becomes my stark belief. A man or a woman should not be the slave of life, or rather of its conventions. One should not be irrevocably bound to any wheel. If you do not like – there's no need for a stronger term – the rut you run in, there should be no circumstances big enough to keep you in that rut.'

'We won't follow you that far,' said Leng; 'but it is certain that courage pays in facing most issues. One might say that if a certain step requires courage that step is worth taking.'

He spoke to me, but his eyes were not on me. Agnes de Burc broke into a low peal of laughter – laughter that was playful, mocking, and, at the same time, touched with bitterness.

'Lady,' protested I, 'don't be mocking us with your laughter, except it be the laughter you laughed at me and my goat a while ago.'

'I was not laughing at any of you,' she denied, 'only at the way you make your arguments fit your – well, your virtues.'

'That is what arguments are for,' said Murray. 'King and Leng are entirely wrong, of course. If what you would like to do does not coincide with what is right, you should at least think twice.'

And here the bored Mrs Daire interrupted, and the talk became the ordinary trivial babble of good society until the ladies left us.

I was in the middle of a long Havana when Lady Clunas came in to say goodbye. She had been very quiet through dinner, but her eye had wandered restlessly and, no doubt, had transmitted certain facts or assumptions to her well-balanced little brain. She now pleaded the long moorland road before her, and turned to me.

'Can I give you a lift as far as the Carr-fork, Tom?' she invited.

'You can, and welcome, Lady Mary,' I accepted, though I should have liked to stay a little longer. But no one pressed me to stay, so I said goodbye and went.

'Agnes and I will be over to see you some of these days,' called Mrs Daire after me.

'By the way, we intend fishing your Loch Ruighi next week,' said Leng. 'I am told the trout are very game.'

'If you know where to find them. You should get Archie MacGillivray to show you.'

'That's the long customer whose boat I hired? He can be hired himself, I suppose?'

'He cannot, then. He is anything but a hireling.'

'He knew how to charge for his old tub, at any rate.'

'That is because you set out to hire it. He comes of a proud race, and if you treat him accordingly you'll find him worth knowing. Good evening, and thanks – for everything.'

I sat by Lady Mary's side smoking my good cigar to its last half-inch, and watching her capable small hands on the steering-wheel. The rattling old flivver made all the noise that was necessary, and for three miles we scarcely exchanged a word. Neither of us liked shouting.

At the fork of the roads, close by where the waters of the loch made little ripples on the gravel, I got out, and Lady Mary switched off her engine. She looked over the wheel straight ahead, and said nothing for a while.

'Dear lady,' said I, 'red hair and and all, you are a great

peacemaker. Yesterday I would have cut Mr Leng's throat in two places, and today I have eaten his bread and salt.'

'And what do you think of him today?' she asked.

'I could not be telling you all of it. He is not a man of my race or of yours. He comes out of Nineveh, or Babylon, or Palmyra. You know, that big, high-shouldered, narrow-hipped race with a glossy wave of black hair, moulded lips, and heavy jowl – a great and relentless breed: he is of that race. My forefathers and his fought always, and we destroyed them because they were too proud.'

'He is no Jew.'

'He is not. He is very different from any Jew. His people held the Jew captive at any time it was worth while. The Jew, though an oriental, was always slave to his women-folk: this man's race was slave to no woman.'

'Perhaps not, but, all the same, Edward Leng is very much in love with Agnes de Burc.'

She said it calmly, who had such a wholesome respect for the proprieties.

'I was thinking the same,' I said; 'but you know. And does she love him?'

'I don't know that.'

'You do not. You cannot read your own sex.'

'And what do you think?' She leaned sideways, her gauntleted hand on the door of the car.

'I haven't started to think, lady. Maybe she is only Semiramis: with luck and brain she may be Aspasia: I hope that she will not be a Deirdre of the Gael – and know tragedy.'

'And the Assyrian a Naisi to your Deirdre?'

I put my big hand on hers. 'Go away home, redhead, before it gets dark,' I said.

'Very well. Was not that Mrs Daire a disgusting woman? Crank up the car, will you.'

'An honest simple body really, and rather likeable.'

I cranked the car, and she went away between the brown slopes, a bonny, small, red-haired young woman that I had somehow failed to understand. Myself I strolled down the road by the lochside, smoking my pipe to keep off the midges. All about me the twilight gradually deepened; and, but for the faint hum of the insects and the shuffle of my brogues in the dust, there was no sound at all over that land.

'It is not improbable,' I soliloquized as I went, 'that woman knows when a man is in love – with another woman. Lady Mary tells me that the Assyrian is in love with the white lady. He may well be, and a queer, strong love that love would be. If I were in love, Lady Mary would see that too, and she would tell me in the direct way she has. Therefore it is certain that I am not in love, and I do not know anyone at all who is in love with me. What falling in love is like I do not know very well, or I might fall in love with Agnes de Burc. It would be a good thing to do, maybe, for it might save her from Edward Leng – and again it might not. Men like that man are great lovers, and the greater for a little opposition. I do not forget, of course, that he is a married man. That is a fact that does not weigh greatly with him, I am thinking; and how it weighs with the lady, only God Himself knows. I know it weighed little with all the women that became great courtesans. 'Tis God that must be smiling at me for thinking that I was a little different from most men in this matter of loving. I am not a bit different, and I am beginning to find that out. It is no wild man I am at all, but a plain household man, who is beginning to think of a woman about the house and the voices of children at play. Thundering red flagstones of hell!'

I stopped in the dust of the road and looked across the dim-shining expanse of loch to the sweeping curves of hill that stood out dead-black and eternally quiet against the pale glow of the northern sky. Out of earth or sky came no smallest sound. Eternity could be no stiller.

'It is here, if nowhere else, that a man should live in peace,' I said; 'but the mind of man, or the blood in him, or the lust, will not let the man be at peace anywhere. But above imaginings and above blood and above lust there is the little white flame of reason that makes us men, and to that small flame I will trust till it is drowned in madness.'

So I went up the hill to the silent cottage that was not yet lonely, to my goat and my bees and my books, and as I went I hummed a small fragment of song by a man I knew:

Had I fashioned all the roses that ever bloomed in June,
The marigold, the daffodil, the heather, and the broom,
The shy leaf-hidden violet, and *canna-bawn* ablown,
I'd long for still some wee small bud whose seed was never
    sown.

Had I choice of all the queenly ones that ever troubled man –
Helen, Cleopatra, and Mary's mother Anne –
I'd sell my choice for ae bawbee and gang the road my lone,
For the quoine was never born I would care to call my own.

But behind that song was no longer the old careless confidence of the heart-free maker.

CHAPTER IX

Though it was the first grouse drive of the season, the birds came down on the butts at a speed that was most disconcerting to my small skill. That was because there was a following wind. In spite of all Archie MacGillivray's coaching, I never could be even half sure of bringing down a bird coming slap at me.

'It is no harder than suppin' kale,' said Archie. 'There is the bit bird – big as a house – maybe fifty yards out, and coming hard at ye, but dead straight. Put the gun on him, left arm well out, throw up the front sight as fast as you are able and let go, and there is the puir thing "clump" on the facing of the butt. That's all there is to it, Mr King.'

That was all there was to it so far as he was concerned. He rarely failed to bring his bird 'clump', sometimes into the butt, but my failures kept on being nicely consistent. I was not disheartened or ashamed. I did get a bird occasionally under difficult conditions, and, as Archie usually gillied for me, I had but to hand him over the gun to get my average beyond ridicule. Of course he was with me this first day of the driving season, and satirically watched my efforts in the first two butts. I had a lucky winger in the first and a quite inexcusable blank in the second.

'The next butt is yours, my old scoffer,' I told him. 'And, vainly I know, I pray Saint Francis of the birds that you miss all shots, or, at any rate, the easy ones.'

He did not. He got in both barrels time after time without registering a miss. It looked easy, but to me it was uncanny.

'I'm not knowing how a man could be missing them shots,' said he, and some of them were really great shots. He was enjoying himself. It was of his own desire that he gillied for me, and that he did most industriously and with a nicely calculated deference when in the neighbourhood of the other sportsmen. It was only in a secluded butt that he would consent to try his truly remarkable prowess.

It will be seen that I had progressed well with Edward Leng since our first untoward meeting. That man did not do things by halves, and he took some pains to manifest his acceptance of my worthiness. I was not churlish enough to show that I did not care one way or another.

After the third drive that morning – it was then approaching noon – the whole party was called together by Davy Thomson, who wanted to try fresh ground near Reroppe Lodge. We gathered at the burnside below Aitnoch Hill – Leng, Murray, three or four local lairds, the gillies, and a cluster of schoolboy beaters.

'Had a good morning's sport, King?' Leng greeted me as I joined the party.

'Splendid. Couldn't get my eye in for a while, but Archie here will tell you how deadly we were in the last butt.'

Leng saw Archie for the first time that morning, and seemed surprised. 'Hello, MacGillivray!' he cried. 'You here? Mrs Daire and Miss de Burc are gone round to your place to get the boat. They hoped you would take them on the loch.'

'That is a pity, now, Mr Leng,' Archie said, and he said no more. He was my man for the day, and there was no more to be said. Archie's code was a simple one. He was the complete aristocrat.

'That is unfortunate,' said Leng frowningly. 'The ladies have so little they can do up here.'

It would be easy to contradict him, for there is much the

ladies can do anywhere. Instead, though I fear in no spirit of magnanimity, I came to his aid. 'Mrs Daire has been promising to call on me,' I said, 'and I should not like her to be disappointed. I propose that Archie and myself entertain the ladies. Davy here has enough guns for his butts, and this is a splendid day for the fishing.'

'Sure you won't mind, King?' Leng was much relieved.

'Not at all. I shall enjoy it.'

'Very good of you. You know how it is with ladies?'

I did not. The ladies could fend for themselves, doubtless, and probably it was in no spirit of sacrifice that I set out with Archie to do the gallant thing by them.

On the head of Aitnoch Hill we halted, as was our custom, filled our lungs with the keen, live air, and looked far and wide over water, moor, and mountain.

'There is no boat on the loch,' I remarked.

Archie's telescopic eyes were prying round the shores, and he touched my shoulder and pointed. 'See at the foot of the loch, where our cart-track meets the Barnagh road.'

'I see a gleam of white. That will be Miss de Burc.'

'It will not. It is a man in white coat and a white cap sitting in a motor-car.'

'The chauffeur. Do you see the ladies?'

'I do not. They will be down at the house with Helen, I'm thinking.'

And so we went down the hill with long strides. Right enough, the ladies were in the house. We heard Mrs Daire's loud and cheerful laugh as soon as we opened the door. They were in the parlour, being entertained by Helen MacGillivray. That crofter's wife was a natural Highland gentlewoman, and could, with a splendid courtesy, entertain princes in her spotless, low-ceilinged parlour with its horse-hair couch, priceless old chairs, mahogany table, biblical pictures (including the awful conversion of one Saul of Tarsus), and its ceremonial, white-draped bed.

I think the ladies were glad to see us. They had glasses of mostly-cream before them, and Agnes de Burc leant easily and beautifully across the table, while Helen and Mrs Daire laughed with her. When Helen MacGillivray laughed she had

68

reason for her laughter and liking for the laugh-maker. This was a new aspect of my lady in white and one worth considering.

I introduced Archie, and he bowed like a chief in his own hall – and that is what he was, of course. Though the younger brother, he was Aitnoch, and as Aitnoch he was known in that land of lairds. Hamish and Helen gave him loyal allegiance. 'You are very welcome, ladies,' he said.

'Archie and myself,' I explained, 'have been deputed by Mr Leng to show you the beauties of Loch Ruighi. I am here because Mrs Daire is here, and—'

'We don't want your second reason, Mr King,' said that lady, looking at me rather knowingly. Her words and her look kept me wondering for a while.

'I am sorry we have spoiled your day,' said Agnes de Burc.

'With the loch in such fine condition the day can't be spoiled,' I said not too gallantly. 'I see that you have a good split-cane rod there.'

'But I cannot use it very well.'

'Archie teaches fishing in one lesson.'

'We are in your hands, then. What do you propose?'

'First we will try the fishing. Then we must visit the Wolf's Island and explore the honey-holes where the wild domestic bee stores its treasure – and get stung if we are not worthy. Then Mrs Daire must visit my hermit cave and see my goat Suzanne, and sample the fare we thrive on. After that we might climb Cairn Rua through the pine-wood, and admire the finest view in this part of Scotland – moors and hills and savage valleys, and the blue ramparts of the Cairngorms behind all. Later we can be looking for other things to do if we have a mind.'

'That is a good programme,' said my lady.

It was a good programme. It went well. That is all I will say.

Late that evening, when the sun was down and no breath of air ruffled the quiet stretches of the loch, I pulled slowly homewards over the dim-shining water, wondering at myself, wondering at man – just wondering. I did not break the weight of silence with a song, as was my habit, but kept time to an old snatch in my head:

My love and I were walking,
    And I cannot call to mind
A word she said, a glance she gave,
    Or if my love was kind.
She says I looked with longing,
    And talked of bliss to come,
But that I have forgotten
    Is most confounded rum.
She says I whispered this and that,
    And looked with longing eye,
And was never tired of kissing –
    But now I wonder why.

But, though I said over that old song to myself, I was
beginning to doubt if I ever possessed the hardy, satiric spirit
of the singer who made it.

CHAPTER X

July was hot and still; early August was still hot, but with a
freshening breeze to ripple Loch Ruighi in the later afternoons; but the last week of August was neither hot nor still.
Dull mornings, with fitful puffs of air crinkling the leaden surface of the loch, were followed by afternoons of rising wind –
wind that rose into a squall with a shower in its teeth, sank a
little, and rose again. All night the wind cried across the
heather and moaned amongst the pines, but at the dawn it died
suddenly, and the sullen waters of the loch slowly smoothed
themselves out.

That weather was good fishing weather for hardy fishermen
who did not mind a splash or two over the gunwale. The
Nancy, crooked keel and all, thought little of a capful of wind,
and was the very boat for such weather. She went crabwise
about the loch, seeking out the feeding-grounds of the trout,
and the angry, hurrying little waves slapped her flanks rudely
but harmlessly. Still there came one late afternoon at the very
end of August that made even the *Nancy* turn tail and run.

And on that afternoon Agnes de Burc, Edward Leng, and myself, with Archie MacGillivray at the oars, were fishing.

It was not the first nor yet the second time that Agnes de Burc and I had fished companionably, but it was the first time that Edward Leng was in the boat with us. He had grown tired rather suddenly of slaughtering grouse. For a fortnight, with Murray and the neighbouring lairds, he had been making record bags on the moor, and then, without seeming cause, left Murray and Davy Thomson to conduct the shoots and came fishing with the lady and me. Archie and I did not appreciate his company, but, with Highland courtesy, hid the fact; and neither Archie nor I could gather from word or look of the lady whether to her he was welcome or not. That is the kind of lady she was. Why he came one might wonder. Perhaps he thought that Agnes de Burc was seeing too much of me, but that would postulate a doubt in him as to his own power, and at that time he had no doubts as to his own power over woman or man. He was a self-centred man and somehow not of the Occident. The thing he did he did with all his might and thereafter lost interest, and we of the Occident never lose interest in a thing we have done. Probably he was with us because the grouse-slaughter had lost all interest and because he liked to be with the lady. While his interest in the shooting lasted I do not think that he was ill-pleased that the lady took an interest in the loch, and in Archie, and in me. It was entertainment for her and did not spoil his. That was the kind of man he was.

He had chosen a bad day. Early in the afternoon we embarked at Archie's pier and worked up the shore against the fitful – not yet heavy – puffs of wind to where the Corran burn enters the loch, and where the sturdy yellow trout lurk amongst the reeds. By that time the wind was stronger and steadier, and neither sun nor rift of blue was to be seen. All the moors were dead brown or deader purple; the pine-wood above my cottage was darkest green; the loch had a peculiar leaden sheen and was troubled with occasional white horses, while the tall dry reeds all about us nodded and swung, and were not tired of asking and asking, 'But what came ye out for to see?'

However, the fishing was good and time passed quickly. Starting from the mouth of the Corran we let the *Nancy* drift, broadside to the wind, down the margin of the reeds where the half-pounders were greedy. In time we were driven offshore, and then Archie with stiff, short strokes pulled us back to the burn-mouth for a fresh drift. The lady, under Archie's and my tuition, had learned to cast a passable line, but, as the weather roughened, had surrendered her rod to me and sat on the bottom board in the shelter of the gunwale talking to Archie. Leng in the stern and I in the bow fished industriously. He showed himself a capable wielder of a light rod, and, if anything, was over-careful with his fish. He played them skilfully, gave them line when they asked for it, and would not let Archie use the landing-net until they showed their yellow in exhaustion. There was something cat-like about that fishing that did not appeal to me.

As the wind rose the drifts grew briefer, and all Archie's energy was called into play. He never complained. There was no sweat on his brow, no strain in his alert blue eyes, and his mighty brown hands grasped the oars with easy strength. His short, sturdy strokes with a kick at the end sent the *Nancy* slapping through the little white horses, while Leng waited impatiently at the stern, rod lifted, and long line blown horizontal. At last I spoke. 'We had better make for port,' I called to him. 'Getting too rough for fishing.'

'One more drift,' Leng cried back. 'There's a two-pounder at the stream-mouth that has risen twice to the saltoun.'

He caught neither his two-pounder nor any other fish on that drift. A squall of wind and thin rain came out of the west, and made fishing impossible. We were past the reeds and a hundred yards offshore in less than a minute.

'Get inshore, Archie,' I cried. 'We'll need to hug it homewards.'

'Nonsense!' cried Leng. 'With this wind behind us we can get home across the loch in a few minutes.'

'We can be trying, anyway,' said Archie. 'Mr King, will you take an oar with me? Miss de Burc and Mr Leng will sit in the bow to hau'd her head down.'

There was really no danger. The *Nancy*, as I knew from experience, was not swampable by any following sea, and Archie and myself at the oars had skill enough to keep her running before the breaking white-caps. We flicked her down the loch at a racing pace, and did not get a cupful of water inboard.

'This will be a bad night,' said Archie over my shoulder. 'Look at MacLeod's mantle in the west.' The west was pitch-black, hiding every gleam of the dying day, so that twilight was already deepening the forlorn hue of the white-lashed water. And every moment the wind was rising. Before we realized it we were down on the Wolf's old stronghold in mid-loch, and driving straight on it too. Archie, glancing over his shoulder, was first to see. 'Pull, Mr King!' he shouted, himself backing water. 'Pull! or we'll strike bottom off the point.'

His backing water, my too strenuous pulling, combined with the kinked keel of the *Nancy*, did the trick very thoroughly. The boat swung broadside to the biggest roller I had ever seen on Loch Ruighi, went gunwale under, and pitched us fairly outboard.

Even then the only immediate danger was that the *Nancy* might roll over on us as we struggled. We were not more than twenty yards offshore, and, as the first plunge of the overturn sent me head-under, I touched gravel with my hands. I struggled to my feet in less than three feet of water, shook the moisture out of my eyes, and saw Agnes de Burc's panama on the surface, her head still below it. In a moment I had her by shoulder and waist, braced myself against the waves, and scrambled ashore to the big boulders below the ruined walls. And there I still supported her, one arm round her slim body and her shoulder against my heart. I know that she clung to me.

The others were ashore as soon as we were, while the *Nancy* came in behind us and banged her gunwale wickedly on the rocks.

'Gi'e us a hand with her, Mr King!' roared Archie, plunging into the water at her stern. Agnes de Burc loosed herself from my arm and I stumbled to the bow, Leng at my side ready to help. With a heave we lifted her as a breaker surged beneath, and turned her clean over a big boulder just out of reach of the waves. Then we rescued what gear we could see – a sodden lunch-basket, a broken rod, and a couple of mackin-toshes. And after that we scrambled to the back of the boat and took stock of the situation. Disaster had come so quickly that we had had yet no time to realize what it meant, but we had time now in plenty.

I saw Archie shake his wet brown towsle as he bent over the *Nancy*. I bent and looked with him, and at once saw that one of the rowlocks with a foot of gunwale was smashed clean away. Archie's big spatulate fingers were feeling round the ragged edges.

'Will she take the water?' I asked in his ear.

He shook his head again. 'With the two of us alone I might risk her,' he said. 'No, Mr King. She will be taking us across when the loch is quiet, and that will be the morn's dawn.'

He straightened up, looked across my shoulder at Agnes de Burc and then at me. 'We are on the island for the night,' he said.

'What is that?' cried Leng, who had caught Archie's words.

'A smashed gunwale,' I cried to him. 'She'll not take the water safely till the loch calms.'

'Good Lord! are we marooned, then?' I thought that he was accepting the situation too readily for a strong man. He was without a hat, his black hair was plastered over his forehead, and his strong, big jowl was already blue and tremoring with the chill.

Very clearly Archie and I saw what was before us. We could have no hope of rescue while that gale lasted, and a full gale it now was, no longer rain squalls, but an even, dry rush of air that drove the breath back into our throats. The only other boat about the lochside was my cockle-shell, and that would never ride the sea now running, even if anyone had seen our mishap and had the will to rescue us. We were marooned for the night, and that was an end to it; and having accepted the situation, the only thing to do was to face it.

'Come away out of the wind,' I shouted. 'Give me your arm, Miss de Burc.'

I took her by arm and waist as a matter of course, and went stumbling along below the walls in the spray of breaking waves to where the good Earl of Moray had breached his brother's stronghold three hundred years ago and more. Through this breach we scrambled into the inner courtyard – a quarter-acre of grass broken by little heaps of crumbling masonry, on which, oddly enough, grew clumps of stunted wild gooseberry. Here the gale no longer bustled us, but it was not yet the shelter I sought. I led straight across to the far wall and through another breach. Here there was a space of a dozen yards between the stronghold and the water, and to the left of the breach a great square bastion jutted out boldly. In that space an old ash grew bravely, and between ash and bastion was a perfectly dry and sheltered angle. In there I shepherded our little flock.

'Now,' I said, 'have we a dry match amongst us?'

We had not. We had plenty of matches, but, of course, all were hopelessly sodden.

'We will keep a box of matches here after this,' I said to Archie.

'We will so,' said Archie bitterly; 'and be damned to us!'

That spot was a favourite picnicking ground for fishers and their women-folk. Agnes de Burc, Mrs Daire, Archie, and myself had used it once or twice. In a shell-hole in the wall was our little cache of peats and tinder-dry bog-pine, but not a single match. I looked at that treasure meditatively, my fingers crumbling a wet match head, but no inspiration came to me – no inspiration could come. I fear that I cursed the dumb peats and threw the useless match at them.

Leng, strangely out of character, accepted without question my control of the situation. 'What is to be done now?' he asked.

'We are here until the wind drops,' I told him, 'and that won't be for some hours. We must get all the wet we can out of our clothes.'

I turned to Agnes de Burc. The urgency of the case made me blunt. 'Miss de Burc,' I said, 'you'll have to strip and wring your clothes dry – dry as possible.'

She nodded. She had not spoken a word since the *Nancy's* capsize, and her silence was true to form. Her face was white, but it had never had much colour, and the wet and cold had not weakened, but rather accentuated the strong bones of cheek and jaw. She had taken off her hat, and her wet clinging black hair curled at the ends.

'Come, you fellows!' I cried. 'We'll strip in the bailey.'

From the breach I turned. 'Take off everything,' I warned

her, 'and wring hard. Then put on some under-things. The others I will re-wring with my horny hands.'

We men were, of course, sopping wet. A few hours like that would not matter to the weather-tough hides of Archie and myself, but they might matter a great deal to Edward Leng. There was somewhere an Eastern fibre in the man, and he softened strangely in the cold and wet. His face was bluish – not ashen – and the jowl, usually so strong, was now merely fleshy. There seemed to be no strength of bone to stand out grimly where grimness was needed.

We stripped quickly, rubbed and slapped ourselves dry, pranced about a little, and proceeded to squeeze the water out of our clothes. Leng stripped well, and his splendidly-muscled torso contrasted with the stringy leanness of Archie, but yet I knew that the force stored in that leanness would, if called on, rend the other's mighty muscles. With blood again running warmly, I resumed my old flannel trousers, homespun jacket, and unlaced shoes. Shirt and stockings I wrung and re-wrung and wrung again, and then impaled them securely on a clump of stunted gooseberry bushes where a current of the gale whirled through a breach in the walls. Archie, without direction, did likewise, and the salved waterproofs we treated similarly. There was no rain any longer; and the wind, like all autumn winds, was not really cold.

'We have at least six hours before us,' I told Leng, 'and we have to get Miss de Burc safely through them.'

'My God! It will kill her – this cold,' he said in dismay.

'It will not. It is more likely to kill you. If you let it get into your bones you'll be dead in a week. You'll have to keep moving this night, Leng, for, if you huddle up and get numbed, you'll have pneumonia. Leave the lady to Archie and me, grown tough in this climate. Come on!'

We went back to our woman. It was almost dark then, and I saw her, a slim, white sapling against the trunk of an old ash. I took her dress – a thin woollen texture – and wrung the last drop of water out of it, and helped her to slip it on. She shivered a little under my hands.

'My dear,' I said, 'this will not do. We'll have to take stern measures if you start shivering.'

'I am not cold,' she told me.

'Let us be comfortable, then,' I said. 'For your own sake you will be clay in our hands and we will put a little life and warmth into it.'

I led her into the angle between rock and bastion. There I sat down, my back against the wall, and gently pulled her down on my knees; and I directed Archie to sit close behind, so that her shoulders rested against him. I slipped my left arm round her waist, and again felt a little tremor run through her.

'No catching chills,' I admonished her. 'Let me feel your hands.'

'But I am not cold,' she again said lowly.

'Then we must make you a little warmer. You must do as you are told for this night, my lady.'

Her hands were very cold. I covered them with one of mine, threw open my old brown jacket so that my chest was bare, and pulled her round so that she almost faced me. As I drew her hands forward she resisted for a moment, and then yielded with a little sudden intake of breath. For I placed her cold hands on my body under my arms – and I did not feel the cold. Her hands moved a little, and were still; and, her head being against my shoulder, I heard her long sigh.

'This is – too exquisite,' she whispered. 'What life-force you have, you strong man – and your skin is like velvet.'

I had no reply to that, but she must have felt the beating of the heart that was warming her and me.

Leng stayed beyond the ash tree and paced up and down without ceasing, for, no doubt, he was frightened for himself. Sometimes he walked slowly, sometimes fast, and again he took little runs back and forth.

'Edward Leng is determined not to die,' I said to Archie.

'He hates the cold,' she spoke, 'but he will not die.'

And so we faced the night.

CHAPTER XI

All night long, without a lull, the great west wind poured overhead, crying in the long grass crowning the broken walls, crashing through the top branches of the old tree, shrieking high over the deep pulsating sough of the driven waters.

About midnight I made the lady take some exercise, and, while she walked up and down with Leng, Archie and I climbed back into the courtyard. We found shirts and waterproofs reasonably dry.

'I doubt I'm no' getting my good flannel shirt to wear,' said Archie.

'You'll thole as you are,' I told him. 'After this night you'll treasure this old grey-back as sacred.'

We went back to our shelter, and I directed Agnes de Burc to take off her dress and slip on my shirt. She protested, laughed and obeyed. Then we bundled her in the waterproofs, and seated her comfortably in the angle of the wall.

'And now, my lady, I am taking off your stockings,' I told her; and that thing I did.

Her feet were cold, and I chafed them between my big palms till they were warm. I saw the white gleam of her skin through the dark, and the more-than-velvet softness of it brought my heart into my throat with a feeling that was akin to grieving. Her feet warm, I wrapped them in Archie's flannel shirt, and thereafter took my seat at her side. As I sat she leant forward on me just a little. Archie sat at her other side.

'Now we shall do,' I said, 'and dawn can come when it is ready.'

'I am as warm as toast,' she said, and there was a lightness in her tone that was not often there. Always was there a grave quietude about that woman, but I think that, as she sat there wrapped up against the cold, she was no more than a young maid happy in the thought of the clean care that men were taking of her.

All that night we talked without end. Sometimes Leng leant

against the tree, listened, and put in a word; and then the dank chill drove him to his pacing and his arm-flapping. These he persisted in with a characteristic self-centredness. I got Archie to talk in his deliberate Highland way of things that were old and of things that were not so old. He told us tales of the royal and terrible old Wolf of Badenoch, and from these went on to speak of the veritable four-footed wolves that once infested the province of Moray; and he told us the saga of the last half-mythical, great wolf in all Albion, and how it met its death at the hands of a man of his own clan – one Donald Ian Mor, a hero in the tradition of Finn and Cuchulain. And that got him to the subject of his own great clan, and of clans not nearly so great; for, to hear him speak, there was only one great clan amongst the Gaels, and that the MacGillivray.

'He is as proud as a Spaniard,' I told the lady.

'Do you know Spain?' she asked.

And forthwith I told her something – not all – of my wanderings in that great land – a land that will be always great: of Seville and Valencia and the long valley of the Madura, and of the folk who peopled these places, and of the heady brown wine stored in the tall earthen jars in the cellars of the white houses by the riverside.

'You have wandered, then?' she asked.

'I have wandered a good deal,' I told her, 'and shall yet. I have yet to see the grey, windy towers of El Greco and the thin water of the Manzanares "where the maids spread their clothes out to dry". A donkey – mouse-coloured and with a black cross – will I buy at Cadiz or maybe Seville, and I will ride at ease across all the Sierras down to San Sebastian, or even Bilbao, where the tramp steamers lie. One companion would I like on that crooked, careless road.'

'And who would that companion be?'

'I do not know yet. There is a long Irishman that I have in my mind, and – you would make a good companion yourself.'

'It is good of you to say that, but I think that our roads are fated to run apart – and not to touch again – ever.'

'They have gone side by side for a month.'

'A pleasant month, thanks to you – and to Archie here. It has been a happy month, spoiled just a little by envy.'

'Envy of what?'

'Of the life you lead up here. I do not know why you ever leave here to go a-wandering. Indeed, I did not know that you, too, were a wanderer. If I owned your house and your bees and your nimble Suzanne I would not leave them for Spain – or for Paris. I would be a very Ruth with them.'

'I will give you that house, then,' I said, 'you strange woman.'

'Will you?' she whispered.

'I will,' I said quietly, 'because I think that I am falling in love with you.'

She lifted her head and looked closely into my face. 'You must not,' she said, her low voice weighted with fate; and her hands grasped and shook me. 'You must not. You must not.'

'Can I be helping myself?' I questioned her simply, looking into the darkness that was her eyes.

'But you can. I did not know that you – you, too, could fall in love.'

'I did not know either.'

'Nor must you know. Your love is not for me – nor mine for you.'

'That man out there loves you,' I said then.

'I know that,' she said, in her old, calm way.

'And do you love him?' I asked as calmly.

'I do not know.' She paused, and again, 'I do not know'; and then, in the same monotone, 'but I must not love any other.'

There was a finality in her words that silenced me – left me without a single word I could say. She herself was first to speak.

'And I shall never own the house with the room where one would be never lonely,' she said sadly.

'But indeed you shall,' I said warmly. 'Knock at that door day or night and the house is yours, and I will go across and live with Archie, who, with me, will be your guard and your staff. If I am away, even as far as Spain or France or the low lowlands of Holland, you will always find the key on the ledge above the inner door. The porch door is never locked. In the cupboard you will find tea, coffee, sugar, an air-tight tin of biscuits, and the finest heather honey. The lamp will be filled, the fire laid, and matches on the hob. There will be potatoes in the pit, peats in the rick, bog-pine in the porch, and when Archie sees your light he will come hurrying with scones and eggs and a lesson in the milking of Suzanne.'

'I will remember all that like fine singing,' she said, a little tremor in her voice. 'Oh! strong man, I am grateful. But I fear me that I shall never reach for the key above your door.'

'We do not know,' I said. 'The key will be always there.'

Soon then came the dawn, and at its coming the wind died as if turned off by some mighty-handed god. There remained only the sough of the waters slowly smoothing. Before ever we thought of moving, a shout from the loch roused us, and there was Murray, that capable man, and Hamish MacGillivray, Archie's brother, coming in on us aboard my boat. They had been twice round the loch shores during the night, and had finally awaited the lessening of the wind up at my cottage, and they had Leng's car at my pier.

'We guessed your plight,' said Murray. 'If anything worse had befallen, the *Nancy* would have washed ashore somewhere.'

'And anyway,' said Hamish, 'how could the loch be drowning Archie and Mr King?'

'Splendid, and more than splendid!' I said to Agnes de Burc. 'You will be home in half an hour and in a hot bath. Then you will sleep, and wake glad of the adventure. This has been a night, and half a night as well. Let us be going.'

Agnes de Burc, Leng, and Murray went ashore in my boat. Before going, the lady came to where I stood a little apart. Her face was slightly drawn in the stark, toneless, hopeless dawn-light, and her eyes were dark wells into which I looked.

'I will not forget this night and all you have done for me,' she said in a low voice meant only for me. 'Do not think of me but as one passing by, and go on leading your own life.'

'I will do that last thing,' I told her, 'but I will think of you a good deal.'

'Goodbye, then,' she said. 'I am going away very soon. I have decided that only now. I am going away, and you will not see me again – ever.'

'We do not know that,' I replied, her hand still in mine, and holding mine. 'Forget not the key that is always above the door.'

She looked at me very steadily – a wide, sombre, steadfast gaze. Then she slowly shook her head and left me.

When they were gone we got the bruised *Nancy* afloat on a loch that scarcely rippled, and reached my pier without difficulty. Archie came ashore with me, and we stood together listening to the gradually dying purr of the departing car.

'Will ye come up and have a dram?' I invited him.

'No' the day,' he declined. 'I only wanted to ask you – do you want that woman, or was it only that you would be keeping the life in her during the night?'

'I could not be telling you, Archie, and be sure that I was not lying.'

'You have told me enough, then,' he said wisely. 'You could be having her if you liked. The man Leng has no power with her, and I ken that you have.'

'You heard what she said?'

'I did. There is a tie, maybe, but it is not of the heart. You have learned me that life is a naked thing, and I would mind you of it. If you have that woman's heart and the wish for her, you will not let her be bound by any little tie – or any big one either.'

'Archie,' I told him, 'I am spent and done this grey morning. Give me time, and we will face the nakedness of this thing called life.'

Heavy-footed, I went up the hill to my empty house. There was a dull weight on me, body and soul. I was tired – tired, and before my mind was a blank wall. I slung my hammock and lay down, and I slept and slept and slept. And I had no dreams that I remembered in waking.

CHAPTER XII

It was already evening when I awoke. The sun, far down in the west, shone aslant into the porch, and one narrow beam came in through the open door, ran across the floor, and climbed up the wall behind me. My eyes followed it and left it for the black rafters overhead, and I lay there wide-eyed, and slowly recalled all that had happened during the night on the island. As usual I soliloquized reasonably.

'Let us look at this thing very calmly,' I said. 'Am I in love at long last, or am I not? It is held by all accepted authorities that this disease of love can be self-diagnosed – indeed, that it does not call for diagnosis, but rather that the smitten one recognizes the malady at its first onset. In that case—'

I got no further with my judicial system. The clink of a shod shoe on the stones outside the door came to my ears, and a man's shadow was cast into the porch. I lifted on an elbow, and, before the visitor could knock, called to him. 'Come away in!' I cried. 'Come away in!' I thought it was Archie.

But the tall man that bent his head below the lintel was not Archie, but Norman Murray from Reroppe. I was surprised to see him, and on surprise followed a touch of anxiety, for almost at once my mind leaped to the possibility of some mishap at the lodge. Had Agnes de Burc fallen ill after her night's exposure? Leng I did not think about at all.

'You had a good long rest,' he greeted me.

'Only just wakened,' I admitted; and then, as lightly as I could, but with watchful eyes on his face, 'and how are my comrades in misfortune?'

'Quite well, so far as I know. I have not seen them since morning.'

'Still pounding their ears, no doubt.'

'They are not,' he said almost casually. 'They are gone away.'

I had been leaning on my elbow, and slowly I let my shoulders sink back to the hammock. I was not stunned, or shocked, nor surprised in any way, though I knew in every fibre of me that this was a momentous piece of news. My only sensation was as if my heart had slowed down, had become subdued, had retired to some remote secret place where it pulsed slowly, emptily, without any relation to the body it kept alive. And at the same time something warned me to take this news calmly, to diagnose it, probe it, observe it from all angles as Murray and I talked.

'They are gone away,' said he.

'They went suddenly?' was all I said in reply.

'Surprisingly! There was a note left for you – from Miss de Burc, I think: it is her handwriting. I brought it over to you.'

He walked across from where he had halted just within the door and handed me a sealed envelope. It was addressed to me – Tom King, Esq, Loch Ruighi – in an upright, round-looped hand that I now saw for the first time. Murray stood at the hammock-side, and I felt his eyes on me intently. I looked up at him over the letter, and he stepped back rather hastily. Somehow I got the impression that he keenly wanted to know what was written in that note.

'It was good of you to bring this across so promptly,' I said.

'Not at all. Never mind me; read your letter if you want to.'

'No hurry,' I said off-handedly. 'It will be a letter of thanks for some fancied favour of last night. Won't you sit down? I had better tumble out.'

'Stay where you are if you're comfortable. I'll rest for a few minutes and toddle back.'

He went and sat at my desk below the window, and the evening light came in and showed me his face clearly. Always a lean face, it was now a tired and haggard one: the face of a man usually austere and composed, but now maintaining composure with difficulty. When he spoke, the careful casualness of his words helped to show the rein he was holding on himself. 'You know, King,' he said, 'I did not know they were going, and I did not know they were gone until an hour ago.'

His very tone was one of excuse, as if I might reasonably blame him for that departure.

'Nor will you know where they are gone?' I questioned.

'To Inverness in the first place; after that—' He threw an

84

arm wide and went on, 'They took your advice this morning: had a hot bath and went to their rooms to rest. I had arranged a grouse drive, and was on the moors till barely an hour ago. When I got back I found a note from Leng telling me that his aunt, Miss de Burc, and himself were off on a cruise for a few days or weeks. These were his words: a few days or weeks. That was all. You know we came up from the Solent in his yacht, which has been anchored off Fortrose. They are at sea by now.'

'Not unless they are in a tremendous hurry.'

'They left Reroppe by motor before midday; they were in a hurry, don't you think?'

'It seems so, indeed.'

Murray leant back in my writing-chair. One arm was thrown forward on the desk, and his gaze concentrated frowningly on his clenched hand. 'I do not like this business,' he said in a low voice, as if speaking to himself.

'What!' I cried. 'The business of Miss de Burc, Leng, and his aunt rushing off on a cruise?'

He nodded his head without turning.

'Is not Leng rather noted for his abruptness?'

Murray did not reply. He sat, head forward, as if communing with himself, and when he did speak he used a reasoning monotone that was strangely disarming, notwithstanding the, to me, intimate subject he broached. 'You have known Agnes de Burc for a month, perhaps,' he said, 'and have been pretty intimate with her during that time. She was rather intrigued with your way of life and your way of looking at life, and last night on the island, out there, you did a good deal for her, I gather, and with a direct simplicity that made intimacy very natural and very splendid.'

He paused, and I placed my hands under my head and gazed at the black rafters. 'I suppose all that is so,' I admitted, to help him out.

'I do not think,' he went on, 'that anyone knowing Agnes de Burc for a month, as you have known her, could escape her charm, glamour – whatever you care to call it – the vital force that is in her and is her – could escape falling in love with her – and no easy love either.'

85

'There is no fool like an old fool,' I said, at a loss to say anything. 'You have known her longer than I have.'

That was a hard, ugly thing to say to him, but he answered it very simply. 'Man,' he said quietly, 'I would give her my immortal soul to play with. Would you do as much?'

'I would not,' said I, 'though last night when her hands were on me I told her that I was falling in love with her.'

His frankness tore that confession from me, for self-revelation is not easy to me.

'That was your way of putting it, and no doubt it was a miracle of understatement. But it was enough to drive her to this last step, which is a bad step, I assure you.'

'Would you tell me why you think that?' I asked him, copying his own quiet tone for good reason.

He laughed a little, short, mirthless laugh. 'For once I am inclined to be over-talkative,' he said. 'But we are both in the same boat, and can at least be frank with each other. Briefly, my dear King, you and I have lost Agnes de Burc, and Edward Leng has won her.'

'I can't go that length with you.'

'You may. I know Edward Leng.'

'And so do I. I know that Eastern man to the marrow of his bones.'

'You may know the man, but you do not know the circumstances that make this thing that has happened so disturbing – tragic – beastly, man, I tell you. Do you know that he is married?'

'Lady Clunas told me that. He and his wife live apart.'

'Yes! You can take things quietly, King. Leng and his wife live apart, as you say. They parted five years ago. It was then he met Agnes de Burc, and it was then I met her too. Do you know, King, that that woman is ridiculously young? Five years ago Agnes de Burc was only a girl – full of enthusiasm, full of curiosity, ignorant, daring, vital, and dowered with that fatal attraction that draws the best and the worst out of men – the best and the worst, King. And she met Edward Leng then.'

There was a quality of high tragedy in Murray's words, and, somehow, the hopelessness of fatalism took possession of me as I listened.

'Don't let me give you any too dark an impression of Leng,' Murray went on. 'I was at college with him. We roomed together. We were the best of friends. In after years we travelled together and shot together – big and little game – and climbed together in the Alps and Himalayas. He liked me, I know, and I liked him, and I can assure you he was then – and is yet – a man of sterling parts: game, resourceful, tenacious, faithful in trial: a man who stuck things out with you to the bitter end: a man you could trust anywhere in a tight corner. That is giving him only his due. And, to go on giving it, you must be told that as regards woman he is quite unmoral.'

'I judged that,' I put in, as he paused.

'And rightly. Unmoral, mind you. He seemed to have no sense of morality as we know it. He was not a loose-liver in any sense of the word, but if a woman appealed to him she was merely to be won, enjoyed, and discarded. He simply did not understand continence. He married as a youth, rashly and impetuously, and, having grown tired of that tie, did not let it interfere with his pursuit of life or what he called love. In fact the failure of his marriage seemed rather to encourage what we might charitably call his philanderings. And he did possess a terrible and ruthless power of attraction: a force of desire, an intensity that was wholly sincere and all-possessing until victory was won, after which soon followed satiety and carelessness. That is the man in brief for you. Well, that man met Agnes de Burc, and you can see that there followed a mutual infatuation – nothing less was possible. And there you are.'

For a time we were silent, thinking our own thoughts. Calmly enough I contemplated all he had said, and, being no longer a romantic youth but a grown man with some claim to a hardly-acquired philosophy, I could not help arriving at a logical conclusion. Bluntly I put that conclusion to the test. 'Tell me,' I asked him, 'is she his mistress?'

'No!' he cried. 'By God! no.' And he hit the desk with his clenched hand. Then he went on very quietly, 'But she soon will be, and you will be to blame.'

'You have hinted as much already,' I said. 'Why?'

He went on as if he had not heard me. 'I know that Leng

obtained some power over Agnes de Burc during that first infatuation five years ago. What it was – great or imaginary – I do not know. I dare not know. I have always refused to contemplate it. But, whatever the power, it was enough, in her own high code – a very high code, King – to make her adhere to the standpoint that no other man had any right to her. There she is immovable. Do I not know? Have I not pleaded with her on my own behalf? She likes me too. With simple frankness she has told me that she will marry Leng when he is free – when he is free, by heavens! Leng has no scruples, of course. He would have taken her any time these five years in the face of the whole world. He is deeply in love with her, as I know, and that is evidence enough for me that she is not yet his mistress.'

'Unless she has qualities that some women – courtesans and others – had.'

'And dominate him permanently. I have thought of that too. But Leng is too self-centred to be dominated permanently. He is not the usual type of lover. He is not in the least jealous of her other admirers, and there are many. He is too confident either of his own powers or of her scrupulous code. He knows my feelings also. It has made no difference to him. Indeed, I have clung to him like a twin-brother. There has not been a day of these last years that I have not known the whereabouts of Agnes de Burc and Edward Leng, that I have not hoped to save her the last irrevocable step. And now—'

He slapped his hand on the table and was silent.

'And will you tell me how I am to blame?' I again asked him.

'I am telling you,' he said, and went on. 'Things carried on without a crisis until our sojourn up here and till our rather odd meeting with you. As I said, you made a strange impression on her. Your life and philosophy pleased her, your treatment of her was something new and very pleasant – a sort of easy comradeship without thought of reward. I tell you, King, that I was damnably jealous, but I was also glad, and that's to my credit. I saw a way out. Here was an attraction that might outweigh Leng's power. And that very thing it was doing, I believe. Whatever happened on the island last night – and you know – to me it is clear that she then realized that you had become important to her. Imperceptibly you had drawn near the closed door of her heart, and it required something elemental to show her the place you held. And there her code intervened. For, if no man but Leng had any right to her, she had no right to any other man. She could not take where she had nothing that she could give. And so, frightened and distraught by the sudden knowledge of her own heart, she has desperately taken this last step. She has gone off with Leng.'

'And with his aunt,' I added.

'And with his aunt, who, poor butterfly, can be dropped at Leng's convenience. That is all I have to say.'

'It is enough,' I said.

'Meaning that you wonder why I have said so much?'

'You'll have your reasons.'

'A simple reason enough, King. Do not think that it has been easy for me to open my mind to you. It has been the hardest thing I have ever done. But, since you and I are the only ones that can help Agnes de Burc, I could not ask your help until you knew what I know.'

'Help!' I cried. 'How can we help or hinder? They are gone and how are we to find them on the broad of the sea?'

'There is that letter I brought you,' he said quietly.

I started. The letter was in my hand under my head, and I had forgotten it for the time. I sat up in the hammock and looked at it thoughtfully. Then I tried to wipe all expression off my face, tore open the envelope, and drew forth a single sheet of notepaper. By nature I am secretive. I could then imagine no urgency that would force me to reveal to another such things as Murray had just revealed, and if that letter contained anything that touched intimately the woman and myself I could and would give no sign. This is what was written:

DEAR STRONG MAN, – I am going away. After all that you were to me last night, I must not stay and meet you. I have no right. You told me, and I must believe you, that you were falling in love with me. Why? why? You must not. And in order that you shall not I must tell you what I am about to do. I am going away with Edward Leng. We are going by sea to the south of France; in a month we shall be in Paris, and that, and for all time, will be the end of me as you knew me. That is all. Go on living your own fine, clean life, and forget your poor, worthless—

Agnes de Burc.

I did not lift my head; I did not move a muscle. Nothing moved but my heart, that beat as slowly and as heavily as a muffled drum.

'Well?' interrogated Murray patiently.

I do not know whether my voice showed any trace of emotion as I forced myself to reply. 'A few words – thanks and farewell. They are gone away – for good – on a cruise.'

'Where? Does she say where?' He was no longer patient.

'By sea to the south of France, and then to Paris. That is all.'

'It is enough.' He looked at me very intently. 'What shall we do, King?'

I did not answer at once, but my thoughts were busy – busy and strangely clear. At last I spoke. 'Nothing,' I said. 'Nothing. She went with him of her own free will and of set purpose. There is no sudden impulse in this thing she has done. She will not be changed by you, or by me either.'

Murray rose to his feet. I fear that he was sadly disappointed in me. 'I am obliged to you, King,' he said quietly, 'for the information contained in that note. It is what I came here for. I'll clear out now if you don't mind. Goodbye.'

He walked across towards me, and I thrust the letter into the breast pocket of my pyjamas. I would not let him see it for all the plains of heaven. 'Won't you have something before you go?' I invited. 'Tea? It won't take a minute to make you some.'

'No, thanks,' he said, his hand out; 'dinner will be waiting me.'

'Have a drink, then.'

'Thank you. I would like a drink.'

I swung out of my hammock and got my whisky. I poured him a stiff four-fingers and a like drink for myself, and added water sparingly. 'Here's to ourselves,' I said; 'the poor spent ones.'

We drank those stiff drams in one deep gulp, and then some

sudden impulse made me hurl the empty glass into the open hearth.

Murray laid down his glass and looked at me curiously. 'What are you going to do?' he questioned.

'Nothing. Nothing at all. But the key of this house will always be above the door.'

'Meaning what?'

'I hardly know. What will you be doing yourself?'

'I know. I am going to Paris. Do you know the Gare de Lyon? The big cheerless station where the trains from the Riviera come in?'

'I know it.'

'So do I. And I shall know it better.'

'Every man must do what he has to do,' I said. 'You will not be rash.'

'I shall be very circumspect,' he said. 'Thanks for that drink, King. Goodbye now.'

We grasped hands, and he left me alone in the room where one should not be lonely. I went back to my hammock, and night found me there, and the rising wind blew forlornly across the heather. And I was lonely.

CHAPTER XIII

Fate, or Chance, or Providence does not play a fair game with us men. It does not abide by any rules, is not moved by any considerations, is not turned aside by any prayers, or made malignant by any curses. Its onset can neither be retarded nor hurried, tempered nor envenomed, avoided nor waylaid. Why blame it? It is we who make the rules of the game, who plead considerations, who shelter behind situations. Why blame it if we are thin-skinned, if we are unready, if we are cowards, if we are fatuous enthusiasts? All we should know is that there is no shield, no armour, no antidote. Some of us trust in fortitude, some in fatalism, some in a hereafter, and a few hardy ones in a grim, derisive, humorous cynicism. And at the bitter end of things our trust fails – and it does not matter.

All that I found out for myself while the barb was twisting in me.

'I never sought the lists of Chance,' I wondered; 'never tangled myself in the meshes of Fate; did not dare Providence to a fall. Here in my small house below the pines and above the water, with the quiet brown hills brooding all around, and the blue, high ramparts of the Grampians behind all, one might hope for ease of heart and serenity of mind. I had them, and now have lost them, and cannot regain them by any volition of my own. Indeed, having lost them, I have not the will to wish them mine again, and thereby lose what the losing brought to me. Meantime, let us go on living, knowing that serenity may return, or even a worse blow, and still hoping that there may remain the spirit that can lose serenity without tears, and accept other and worse blows with philosophy.'

And again I told myself:

'In a little while now I will leave this place and seek Spain, where the sun is warm in October, and I will help to judge the qualities of the new wine and the maturing of the old. A donkey will I have too, and ride on it across the Sierras, and across the Manzanares, and into the land of the Basques, and the proud and courteous people of all that land I will know and acquire wisdom from. But I shall have no companion to ride with me on that twisty road, for, yet awhile, I am not fit companion for any man.'

And that set me thinking again of one woman.

I stayed on at Loch Ruighi, and the key of my house was ever above the door. Neither did I shirk the ways of life I knew. I went on the moors with Davy Thomson, on the loch with Archie, and gave a hand to Hamish MacGillivray with his harvest, which was very early that wonderful year. How long I might have stayed I do not know, but after a fortnight I received a letter from Neil Quinn, and that letter changed all my plans – changed everything.

'Look where I do be, long man,' he wrote, 'at Uiskavagh, Isle of Skye, on the shores of Loch Eyndale, that runs and winds from the open sea that Stevenson wrote songs about – Skye and Mull and Canna and Eigg and Rum, and Barra low down on the horizon – as famous an archipelago as any in song or story. All about me are the wine-red moors and over every prospect tower the wonderful pinnacles of the mighty Cuchullin Hills. For the sake of the Lord God Almighty come you over and see life with me. And, unlike Kipling, you don't need to buy no 'am neither. There be fish in the waters greedy for mussels: whiting, the chicken of the sea, codling fresh-bearded, haddock marked by Peter's thumb, and torpedo-tailed mackerel; there are lochs in the hills – hills like your own and lochs not as big as Ruighi – stocked with Loch Leven trout and rainbow-trout and sea-trout that have been transplanted; there are coneys amongst the limestones on the brae-faces, and red grouse on the moors, and blue hares a-plenty. Also there is a motor-boat, double-keeled and with a most entertaining engine. And above all there is the whisky – Uiskavagh whisky, the finest whisky in the world when drunk in Skye; old as a grown man, mild as your goat's milk, soothing as a woman's hand in your hair, inspiring as a tune – a very great whisky. I have my fiddle too, and a battle-song of John Lom's:

By the shore of Inverlochy,
In the snow at Inverlochy,
In white frost foam at the edge of Linnhe Loch—

'And I have a spate of talk that will confound all your heresies and make you a saint at the end of your days. Bring a trouting-rod with you. Mine reached me all right – thanks for sending it. I would like to meet again that black-avised patrician that used us so hardly on Leonach side. Have you anything more to add to that history? Alistair Munro, that stout fellow, is up in the grey lands of Caithness amongst his own clan, serving his country in a humble way and poaching his laird's salmon with prodigality.

'I shall be here for a full month and shall be able to house you royally. The distillery officer is on leave, and I am doing duty for him. He has loaned me his house, his garden patch, and his motor-boat, so that I – and you – may not suffer as we deserve in the small house they call an inn, where the staple diet is salt herring, fresh whiting, and a flavour of peat. I cook ham and eggs to perfection; the mutton is the best in the islands; and rod and gun yield luxuries galore. Wire me when you are coming, and I will meet you at Portree with the old Rudge.'

There was an invitation that no live man could treat lightly. It pulled me out of the rut I was like to get bogged in. It gave me a perspective of things worth a closer view. Therefore I stored my cupboard with tea, sugar, coffee, biscuits; I subjected my hives to a final robbing for the golden heather honey; I filled the lamp, laid the fire, and placed matches on the hob; my potatoes were already stored; there were fresh peats in the rick, and dry wood in the porch. Finally, I locked the inner door, and placed the key on the shelf above it. 'All that is now useless,' I said, 'but a promise is worth keeping.'

Then I crossed the loch and sought Archie MacGillivray. 'You will take charge of my goat Suzanne,' I told him. 'I am going to the Isle of Skye for a month with Neil Quinn.'

'Good!' said Archie, and he was pleased, I saw. 'Good! and twice as well. But don't be letting that wild man lead you astray.'

'Listen you, now,' I instructed him. 'Every evening before you go indoors, and again before you go to your bed, look you across the water to my cottage.'

'I will do that,' said Archie. ' 'Tis what I do always.'

'If you see a wisp of smoke or a light, take eggs and scones—'

'And a lesson in the milking of Suzanne,' he carried on.

'You know your piece,' I said. ' 'Tis not likely you'll be called on to perform it.'

'One would be wondering sometimes at the things that would happen,' said he. With a great forefinger he scratched his bearded cheek and looked at me inquiringly. 'Tell me,' he put – 'suppose the man Leng comes too—?'

'You are no longer a child to be taught lessons,' I reprimanded. 'You will do the things required of you by necessity and right.'

'I will so,' he said. He straightened his long body, his shoulders hunched themselves, his great hands opened. 'It might be that I would break him in three halves,' said the descendant of Donald Ian Mor. And that thing he could do, too.

'If that has to be your way,' I told him, 'do not invite the

94

parish to see it done. Tie the pieces to a large stone, and sink them in the thirty-fathom hole where the cannibal trout lie.'

'I will be very careful,' he agreed. 'Good luck to you now and on the road, and come back with less lines between your eyes.'

CHAPTER XIV

Next morning, in bracing autumn weather, knapsack on back and cased fishing-rod for staff, I took the road. I had planned for myself a notable tramp over a splendid curve of country, where made roads were few and there was need for the best foot forward. I crossed the wide moors of Clunas, and leaving Nairn on the right skirted the heathery carse of Delnies, and so came to the green and tide-troubled narrows of the Chanonry Ferry by Fort George. Crossing that ferry, I had lunch at the Hawkhill, Rosemarkie, and with renewed vigour faced the hog-back of the Black Isle. Evening brought me to the old town of Dingwall at the head of the Cromarty Firth, and there I stayed the night at the house of a friend. The daughter of that house – a golden-haired Norse maiden – was a friend (or it might be a little more) of Neil Quinn's, and so I was doubly welcome.

On the morning of the second day I faced the hills in earnest – the great hills of the north – and late in the afternoon came down through the deer sanctuary above Loch Beannachan into the head of Strath Conon, where all roads are lost in a welter of immense and silent peaks. That night I stayed at the lodge of Scardroy with the keeper of the deer-forest, an old acquaintance of Quinn's and mine, with whom we had stalked the shy hinds in November. I was gladly welcomed in that remote house, regaled royally, and kept out of bed until midnight talking of the outside and the friends we both knew.

On the third day my walk was not much more than a dander. I said goodbye to the keeper at the head of the watershed by Loch Conmartin, and strolled down the easy braes to the railway station at Achnasheen, which I reached before two in the afternoon. Behind me were fine days of marching – off all made roads, by sheep tracks, deer paths, trackless reaches of heather, and scattered wilderness of granite – marching that few had tried since the quieting of the clans. Now I was at the railway, and had ease in prospect.

At Achnasheen I caught the afternoon mail-train for the Kyle of Lochalsh. Through the very gut of the hills that little train wound its way downwards until it came to the green tide-waters of the long Loch of Carron, and there it twisted and turned by the rocky shores, until at last and very suddenly it shot out into the sunny open and went whistling down into Kyle, that looks across the narrow sound to the great mass of Skye, and is washed by the clean salt waters of the Minch.

The ancient little paddle-steamer was waiting for us at the pier, but our arrival did not hurry its departure. Leisurely it gathered in its complement of cargo and passengers – boxed luxuries for the good folk of Portree, Gaelic-speaking old dames out of Skye for the marketing, and a touring motor-car that had to be manoeuvred aboard over a daring seesaw contrived out of old planks. Finally the engine was levered over a dead centre by a couple of firemen with crowbars, and we squattered through the choppy waters of Kyleakin and out into the broad billows of the Inner Sound. It was a calm and pleasant evening, but some distant flurry on the ocean beyond far Rockall had sent in a mighty swell that took us abeam and tilted us into a crabwise gait that was somewhat ridiculous. The squat little *Glencoe* crawled aslant up the immense but gentle green slope of the swells, and slid crookedly but imperturbably into the quiet valleys beyond.

At Broadford we dropped a little cargo and most of our old dames, and proceeded on a fresh tack to the long iron island of Raasay, with its high trellis-work pier and lofty ore-chutes; and from there we straightened out on the long and final leg to Portree. Our course took us close in below the towering hills of Skye, but the evening mist-curtains already clothed the great red-brown bens, hid the black pinnacles of the Cuchullins, drifted and clung along the brae-faces, and stretched prying fingers into every glen and corrie.

While we were yet a long way down the sheltered harbourage

of Portree I saw, from my post at the bow, the grey and dis-reputable hat of Neil Quinn above the whole population of the burgh congregated on the pier. His long neck outshot the islanders, who are not a small race. I waved a hand to him and saw the flourish of his hat, and soon he was grasping me by the shoulders and reading my face with his shrewdly humorous eyes. One could not help liking the pleasantly sardonic, aqui-line, slit-chinned face of the lad. 'Fine!' he cried. 'Grand! You look fit but thin. 'Tis some bracing up you need, my old stick-in-the-mud.'

'I need a few good long marches,' I admitted. 'I haven't done much walking these last days.'

'Faith, you'll get a fine long march tomorrow if you are not too lazy. Or should I book a seat for you on the mail-cart?'

'Where's your old crock, then?'

'Busted. Broke a valve coming up Glen Brittle. I have wired for another, and it should be here in a few days.'

'Then let us walk. Shall we start now?'

'We are staying here the night. All my purchases are to make – lemons, for instance, and little luxuries for your tender palate. We will send them by the mail-cart, and follow in the morning.'

We went up the town together, easy comradeship between us at once, and none of that first shyness that is present at the first meeting of even old friends.

'This is quite a town,' I wondered. 'I understood that all the houses were "black" houses, and the heather at the door. All these hills about us are green, and there is heather nowhere.'

'Wait you till tomorrow. We have eighteen miles before us where heather is plenty and houses few. By the way, did you have tea on the *Glencoe*?'

'I saw the cook decapitating and disembowelling herrings with an unclean thumb—'

'You were dainty. They eat well aboard the *Glencoe*. Come and let's try a pair at the hotel.'

We slept together that night in a big bed at the MacLeod Arms, because rooms were scarce during the tourist season; but before we slept we talked and smoked and talked and smoked again, our pipes glowing in the half-dark and the words shuttling back and forth. Naturally our talk turned to the Leonach adventure, and I developed the later history of that affair. I had made up my mind to do so, for I wanted to hide nothing from my best friend.

'You did not see a lady on the riverside that day?' I asked him.

'Not to remember. I was too busy making war.'

'If you had seen her you would not have forgotten. She was watching you from the rocks, and watching me lying doggo behind the birch screen. I almost popped into her arms, and was treated coldly. Next forenoon she turned up at my cottage with Leng the big man you fought, Murray his friend, and Davy Thomson carrying my hazel staff.'

'By damn! You were in a hole. This is getting interesting. I suppose the vixen gave you away. Women have no sense of proportion.'

'You are wrong this time, my woman-contemner. She did not give me away; nor did Davy, of course. They had merely tracked the motor-car and your side-car outfit in the dust, and Leng had no more than a suspicion amounting to certainty of my complicity. The whole thing came to nothing, and the lady never said cheep from beginning to end.'

'A strange lady that,' marvelled Quinn. 'She must have admired me in my naked wrath – it would never be wee Alec Munro.'

'It might have been myself—'

'You! You old leather skin! I would like to meet that lady. What was she like – young and pretty, by any chance?'

'It is well for you that you did not meet her. Snort away, but it is well, you poor impressionable Gael! She was young, but not pretty – certainly not pretty. Agnes de Burc was her strange name, and she was unmarried.'

'The Burkes are a Galway clan – a dash of Spaniard, Norman, Gael, Firbolg, and Tuatha Dé Danann,' said Quinn.

'That might well be; she is of no modern blood. She is young and tall and slim – not really slim, but with lines that give lightness. Her very modern dress robes her pagan-like, and shows, despite it, the long, lithe lines of body and limb. Her neck is set well back on clean shoulders, and droops just a little forward. Her hair is black and fine, and, when wet, curls at the ends. Her face is pale, rarely showing any colour; and her eyes are dark, but of what shade I have not yet found out – and never shall. And that is only a bare outline, Quinn, for she is the most beautiful woman I have ever met, and her supreme qualities are a static calmness and some magnetic property that compels the worship of men – all men, Neil.'

'My God!' Neil Quinn whistled. 'Hit! Long Tom King of Loch Ruighi hit between wind and water. How long has this been going on?'

'I have seen a good deal of her, if that is what you mean. For a month, while Leng and Murray slaughtered grouse, she, Archie MacGillivray, and myself fished the loch, picnicked on the island, and dined at my cottage on new potatoes, salt, and goat's milk, with a side-dish of honey. Only a fortnight ago I held her in my arms, and her head rested on my shoulder.'

'Morning star! Tower of ivory! House of gold! pray for us.' His voice showed genuine concern. 'Tom King, are we going to lose you?'

He sat up in bed quickly, and his hand sought my shoulder.

'Lie down, you omadhaun,' I chided him, 'and I will tell you.'

I told him matter-of-factly and rather baldly of the night on the Wolf's island; and, lying without a movement, he listened very quietly, so that I could feel his live mind making pictures and seeing all that I was leaving out. Quinn was no scoffer at bottom, but a youth of considerate and sympathetic instinct, and when I had finished he lay still, without speaking, for a long time. When he did speak he mused aloud rather than addressed me.

'I don't suppose,' he said, 'that any man is immune to certain stirrings of the blood, given certain circumstances. You, without any illusions, are like the rest of us when tried hard enough. Without flattering you too much, I am also inclined to think that the man and the circumstances might also affect the woman.'

He paused for so long that I incited him. 'Go on,' I invited him. 'I like your stilted reasoning. Draw your logical conclusions.'

'Damn it! I am afraid to,' he cried impulsively. 'Tell me the rest, Tom.'

'There is nothing to tell. You seem to have forgotten Edward Leng.'

'Edward Leng! the big man! What of him? Is he a suitor?'

'More than that. She is engaged to marry him when his wife dies.'

'Thunder! This is getting complicated. Does she care so much for him?'

'I don't know. I never asked her that.'

'But did you not pursue the advantage you undoubtedly had that night? Did you not want to?'

'I might have wanted to – I don't know – but I did nothing. The party left Reroppe next day.'

'Oh! You haven't seen her since? Where did they go?'

'I haven't seen her since. They went on a yachting cruise to the south of France.'

'But look here, you sluggard—' he almost shouted, kicking the sheets impatiently.

'Easy, Neil! Easy!' I soothed. 'Take it easy, boy. It was no more than a passing incident in a long life. I assure you that the woman has swung clear of my orbit, and is not likely to cross it again. As you say, I have no illusions, and hope to acquire none. The woman certainly affected me – as I may have affected her – but she is gone, and I am not in my first youth, nor yet such a weakling as to pine for what I cannot have. We will carry on, old boy. I am here to recover, with your aid, the taste for the only life worth living, and let it go at that.'

And we let it go at that. Though the secret places in me objected to revelation I was glad that, albeit lamely, I had explained to my one great friend how things were with me. Had I not done so, our month of fine clean intercourse would have been marred beyond any worth to him or me.

CHAPTER XV

We slept late next morning, and it was nearly eleven o'clock before we set out on our eighteen-mile tramp to Uiskavagh, at the other side of the island. Able footmen that we were, we looked upon it as no more than a stroll between meals, and loitered along easily, smoking a serene pipe and talking by and large. For the first eight miles or so we held to the main road up a wide and breezy valley, with a burn brawling now on one hand now on the other, and with the fading purple of the heather all about us. Where the road begins to drop steeply into the Glen of Sligachan, Quinn turned off to the right on a faintly-defined path in the heather, and from there onwards we went in single file.

'This cuts off a five-mile elbow,' he told me over his shoulder, 'and brings us down on the footbridge below Uiskavagh.'

He set off at a hillman's pace into a wilderness of low brown hills that narrowed the horizon, and absorbed us in their own silence. Here and there the small saffron-brown island cattle or goat-like black-faced sheep moved aside a little to let us pass, and gazed steadfastly at us as we passed. Occasionally a shining-white sea-bird floated and vanished across the round hill-tops, or a solitary hoodie-crow flapped slowly along the quiet slopes. But for the clink of our shoes on fragments of granite and little sighing eerie breaths of air across the heather there was a great and abiding silence – a silence of old places, ancient as the hills – and it wrapped us round and entered into us, and filled us with peace, and lulled us into a quiet and trackless reverie that took no heed of time or of men or of eternity.

Sometime we won out of that tumbled land of quiet, and halted where the path dropped steeply into the great valley that cuts the island in two. We shook ourselves awake to look. Half a mile below us ran a winding, hurrying river with a narrow green ribbon winding with it, and beyond that ribbon began the true wine-red moors of Skye – moors that ran up and up into immense red-brown hills, beyond which towered the sheer purple peaks of the Cuchullins. And high above all arched a pale-blue sky full of the austere northern light.

Presently my eyes followed the course of the river in its green band, and then I saw the head of Loch Eyndale, that long fiord that winds in and in from the far outer sea and is burnished like a silver mirror. On the northern shore were steep green braes, and on the southern shore a gently sloping cultivated stretch sheltering below high hills. Little slated and thatched houses were dotted here and there.

'Quite a settlement?' I commented.

'Yes,' said Quinn. 'And behind those jutting headlands down the loch are townships of "black" houses all in a lean row, and drawing a steady, secure, and sufficient income from old-age pensions. The young folks grow potatoes and oats amongst the rocks, and catch whiting and haddock for kitchen. What else is needed?'

'You have trees, too,' I said, pointing to a small grove near the waterside.

'The only ones on this side of the island,' boasted Quinn. 'And notice the chimney-stalk of the distillery sticking out of them. Do you see that small slated house on the hither side of the trees and close to the shore? That's the famous inn where we are not staying. And do you see that fine two-storeyed house on the brae above it, just beyond the row of cottages? That is our mansion, and it is designed, I believe, in the Neo-Platonic style!'

'Four walls to the weather and a roof atop. Come on! I am as hungry as a gull, and our dinner is still to cook.'

'Do you notice a wisp of smoke pluming out of our chimney?' queried Quinn as we went down the brae.

'So there is. You don't employ menials, I hope.'

'Not menials. That fire was lighted by one of my tail. Standing in the officer's shoes I own all the distillery and the staff thereof. The fire below that smoke was lighted by Sandy, the still-man, two hours ago. Put an inch to your step, then, and you will see what you will see.'

We crossed the river by a footbridge below the ford, and went along the farther slope by a winding road that in time brought us to our destination. As we went up the footpath across the little flower-garden in front of the solidly-built stone house a supremely delicious odour tickled my nostrils and made my mouth water.

'My soul! There's heaven's own cook somewhere, and I that hungry.'

The opening of the front door gave us a stronger whiff of gently-cooking viands, and we ran the source down in the big, flagged kitchen at the end of a long passage where all the doors were closed. A fine peat fire glowed through the bars of the range, and from within the shut door of the oven came a small sound of roasting.

'This,' said Quinn, 'is our kitchen, dining-room, and living-room combined, and you are very welcome, Mr Tom King of Loch Ruighi.'

'Thank you, Mr Quinn. What have you got in that oven?'

'That you will be seeing. First, I want you to notice my arrangements for our comfort. I have saved ourselves a lot of housemaidery by confining our activities to this kitchen, the bathroom, and one bedroom with a couple of camp-beds. See these comfortable basket-chairs, and this white deal-table with old but clean newspapers for cloth, and admire the shining array of cutlery and delft on the dresser. The bathroom is on the first landing. Go thou and wash, and leave me to my devoirs.'

The cool island water was pleasant, but I hurried over that wash. When I got back to the kitchen the table was laid, and Quinn's long back was bent before the oven. He was withdrawing a large cooking-pan that sizzled forth delight.

'The whisky is on the table,' he said, intent on not spilling the gravy. 'Have an appetizer.'

'I will,' I accepted, 'though I need none. What dish is that?'

He exhibited a beautifully browned mass.

'When I got your wire,' said Quinn, 'I pursued these grouse – a brace of them – with relentless and fatal fury. The rabbits were no trouble, and they are young and tender. I arranged the birds in the centre of the pan, and buttressed them with layers of dismembered coney, butter, and sliced onion – an inspiration all my own. The still-man put them in the oven two hours ago, and I pray the god of little pots that they taste as well as they look and smell. Draw in, my trencherman. The bottle is in front of you.'

That meal was a meal too good for princes, or even popes, but just good enough for two hungry men off the heather. The whisky was worthy of Quinn's fluent praise; the rabbit was as tender as chicken, and had borrowed the flavour of the game, while the grouse had lost none of its own; the gravy was delicious; the bread crisp, though it had come all the way from Glasgow by water; and when finally we lay in our basket-chairs, slippered feet on the range, pipes of American caven-dish betwen our teeth, and cups of black coffee near our hands, we were as content as king or beggar, with no remorse for yesterday and no boding for the morrow.

'It is to be seen that one is going to enjoy oneself,' I said to the ceiling, 'if one has not to work.'

'I was thinking myself,' said Quinn, 'that it would be your turn to wash the dishes in the morning.'

With a speculative eye I looked at the table in disarray.

'We wash up once a day,' explained Quinn – 'before break-fast.'

'I am too lazy to question the injustice,' I said. 'The morning is a long way off. But what will *you* be doing?'

'I will be down at the distillery seeing what work the man-ager can postpone.'

'You do work occasionally, of course?'

'We do. The Glasgow boat calls weekly, and we send out a little whisky to cheer the southrons. If there is nothing doing tomorrow we will go fishing. Can you pull a twelve-foot oar?'

' 'Tis longer than I am used to.'

'At the end of the first mile you think that you will die in one minute or maybe two; at the end of the second mile you decide to go on pulling until you do die; somewhere in the third mile you discover yourself admiring the scenery and the oar swing-ing itself. Tomorrow if it is not raining – and rain is not un-usual – four of us are taking the manager's whale-boat out to MacLeod's Maidens where the big pollack feed, and there is a seven-mile pull in slack water.'

'You will bury me in deep water.'

'We will. Next day we will try the big trout in Sleadale Loch over the hill behind us, but if the day be very fine we might have a wallop at the Cuchullins and a peep down on Coruisk, that dark lost water. I have a bad head for the climbing, and look to you to rescue me from death in the steep places. The following day—'

'You look too far ahead. Where is that fiddle of yours?'

'Right! Let us take our minds off the dish-washing of the morrow's morn.'

And so the talk went.

CHAPTER XVI

It was a fine late-September forenoon after a blowing night, and Quinn and I were taking things easy after a fortnight's strenuous playing. We were in the big grass-grown courtyard that fronted the distillery and ran down to the waters of the loch. The little landing-stage for small boats was just below us at the mouth of the strong burn that gave its power to the distillery plant. Quinn, with blackened hands, and the requisite blacker language, was giving his motor-cycle its final overhaul, preparatory to both of us wrestling on the side-car. Close at hand I was sunning myself at full length, and smoking a contemplative pipe, on the sloping platform used for loading casks. Under my hat-brim I could see the green-blue loch wimpling in the gentle breeze, and could hear the soft, sighing lap-lap of the wavelets on the gravel bank below me. The only other sounds were the occasional clink of Quinn's box-wrench, and the resonant tap of the cooper's mallet as he tested casks in the cavernous warehouse behind us. Tilting my head a little, I could see the steep, grey-green, sheep-dotted braes on the other side of the loch, and above them the delicate, transparent, far blue-green of the sky, flecked here and there by little white clouds sailing. Turning my head to the right, I could see the head of Loch Eyndale with its stretch of black mussel-grown beach, and beyond it the ruddy rolling moors with the wonderful pinnacles of the Cuchullins towering above all. The brilliant sunlight shone on these pinnacles, and they were no longer black but scintillating with colour – red, bright-green, stark-yellow, basalt grey – and in that unusually clear air every cornice and corrie was defined in the sharpest perspective.

'From here,' I said to Quinn, 'I can see the corrie – Corrie-na-Creche – we climbed yon day you lost your head and thought Scuir-nan-Gillean was falling on you.'

'Yes,' he said, without looking up, 'I have no head on a hill, but 'tis maybe better than having no head at all.'

'Like some you know. Still, you went to the top of that cliff and showed me Coruisk, that black lost loch hidden in its chasm.'

'I was braver than you knew that time. It was an ordeal I will not face again, and mark you that! When the whole world is atilt and reeling, and the easiest thing to do is to let go, it is not easy to do anything else. No more precipices for this child. What shall we do this fine day? This old crock of mine will be ready for the road in a minute. There's Dunvegan and the Quirang—'

'Don't rush me! Haste, as you quote, is the attribute of devils. Let us take things easy this day, for I am again in a mood to take things easy. You will be glad to hear that. I fear that I have been suspiciously strenuous in killing time, but now serenity, peace, carelessness, perspective, the dominion of reason over imagination have come back to me, and today I know myself for the first time in weeks.'

'Hold ye fast to that knowledge, then,' advised Quinn, giving me a quick look. 'But if you would stop your blethering and give me a hand with this side car. I might then be prepared to discuss your mental state.'

'No hurry. By the way, my cavendish plug is about done – thanks to you.'

'The manager has a box of Tam o' Shanter that he hoards for emergencies.'

'Then will I seek him in his lair and beg some!'

Lazily I lifted myself to a sitting posture, and there sat leaning on my hands and staring at the loch. 'My certes!' I exclaimed; 'but is she not the beautiful one? Look at her, Neil.'

He straightened, looked at me to get the direction, turned, and was at gaze on the instant. 'Just my dream,' he whispered admiringly. 'A beauty, surely! White as a herring-gull from water-line to heel trucks, and as light on the water for all her eighty feet of length.'

'Eighty feet your grandmother!' I disputed. 'She will be sixty feet from stern-post to bowsprit. You are counting in the line and the dinghy towing astern.'

'Eighty feet over all,' he said stoutly. 'And I lay you she has an auxiliary engine under that stern-house. Man, let's pirate her and go a-sailing to the coasts of High Barbaree.'

'Let's. I'll be capting and you playboy.'

'She is a stranger on this coast,' he observed, too intent to argue his rank. 'See the man at the bow heaving the lead. He need not trouble – there's plenty of water below her keel on that course. Ah! but she is coming round. You had better be careful now, my man – you'll be in shoal water in a minute or less. You have found it, have you? Good! Down runs the sail, and there goes the anchor. Mark you how she checks and bows like a swan, and swings gracefully to the run of the tide. We are going to have visitors, my lad – they are hauling in the dinghy. Who the devil will they be?'

'The devil a know I know,' I said. And I did not. I did not even begin to guess, although she who reads this will know at once that the little yacht that had come sailing up the loch, and was now anchored a quarter-mile offshore, carried Agnes de Burc and Edward Leng aboard. This – call it denseness – on my part will show how well I had patched up my wound, how deeply I had buried what was past and done with, how securely I had sealed a little empty chamber in my heart. A full month had elapsed since that night on Loch Ruighi, and, with an effort that had been very great and very bitter, I had put it irrevocably behind me. And, also, in that month I considered that things had become irrevocable for Agnes de Burc.

'They are coming ashore,' cried Quinn. 'There's at least one lady on board – probably a honeymoon couple.'

Even then I had no least inkling. And here Quinn grasped my arm and pointed. 'We are no sailors,' he said. 'See that flag of theirs. They have trouble aboard.'

The black-and-white pennant was at half-mast, and, now that the sail was down, showed clearly against the green braes beyond the water.

'That looks serious,' I agreed. 'If they are amateur sailors it may be only a bit of carelessness.'

'I hope so,' said Quinn; 'and, anyway, if they are honeymooners how otherwise would a man fly his flag? Here they come.'

The dinghy had pulled off from the yacht's side. There were three people aboard – a jerseyed sailor at the oars, and a man and a woman in the stern. They were within fifty yards of us before I recognized them. I found myself gripping Neil Quinn's arm, and speaking in a voice a little above a whisper. 'See who they are, Neil – Agnes de Burc and Edward Leng!'

He started and looked between narrow lids. 'It is the big man himself,' he whispered back; and he turned his keen young eyes on me. 'Put the mask back on that face of yours,' he said softly. 'You and I, Tom King, can meet any two people on God's earth anywhere – on any ground or none – even if he had horns and she were Dolores. On with your mask!'

For, seeing Agnes de Burc coming in on the water, I found that my hard-won serenity, peace, carelessness, perspective, dominion of reason had clouded over; that the wound in me had still a twinge in it, that – that I was still a man. It was well, indeed, that I had a mask to put on.

I do not think that my face betrayed me as I went down to the little landing-stage to meet them. 'Well! well!' said I lightly; 'we do meet in strange places.'

'Hullo!' cried Leng, in a surprise that was at first wide-eyed and then frowning.

'I heard you had gone cruising,' I said carelessly, even cheerfully, 'but thought ye had sought warmer seas.'

I wondered why it took my light tone to reassure him of something. The frown left his face, and in turn he became cheerful.

'Cruising we were,' he said, 'and warm seas our goal. But, instead, we have had the very devil of a time.'

Quickly and lightly he hopped from the thwart to the stage at my side, and shook my hand frankly. 'Glad to see a known face in these wilds,' he said, and at once turned and reached a hand to the lady – 'Let me help you, Agnes,' he said.

But she was not looking at him – she was not looking at anyone. While the boat had yet been a dozen lengths from the landing she had seen me coming to meet them, and her face showed a startled surprise and some other emotion that I could not name. The blood flamed in her cheeks, ebbed again as quickly, and left her very white and still. And now she sat with her hands lying relaxed in her lap, and her head was bent over her hands. She did not stir. There was an immobility about her that was scarcely human. She seemed sunk in some profound reverie, in some infinite cogitation beyond the very borderland of thought: lost in some far abyss of the mind, so deep that the outer signs of life seemed stilled beyond all waking.

'Come on, Agnes!' urged Leng, his hand still out.

For yet a little space she sat motionless. Then her shoulders lifted in a long sigh, and next instant she was on her feet, her hand in Leng's, and with a lithe ease was on the planking within a yard or two of me. She looked at me steadily – the old, sombre, hooded look of the woman who masks her soul or lays it bare – inclined her head very slightly without speaking, and turned to Leng. I was not piqued at this coldness, yet I said, 'This lady used to know me.' She did not seem to hear.

'Miss de Burc,' Leng spoke for her, 'has had a most unfortunate experience.'

'I am sorry. Your flag—'

'Yes,' he explained; 'my aunt died aboard this morning.'

So that poor spent force had at last ceased to persist. Remembering the genuine, if aimless, kindliness of her I was touched, but I could only repeat myself. 'I am sorry. An accident—?'

'No. I will tell you later; but, first, have you not a hotel in this place?'

'Yes, there is one; but you would probably be more comfortable aboard your yacht.'

'So I tell Miss de Burc, but she prefers to stay ashore – for the present. I am staying aboard.'

I noticed that pause. 'I will show you the inn,' I said.

He called to the sailor to bring the lady's bag, and we went up the yard, Leng in the middle. He glanced at Quinn as we passed, and to Quinn's gesture of salute lifted a hand smilingly. 'One of our young friends?' he remarked in a low voice. 'You may tell him that the hatchet is buried.'

'We have had a beast of a voyage, King,' Leng went on. 'Winds and high seas. My poor aunt used to be a first-class sailor too, but her heart seemed to play out on her – fatty de-generation, I suppose – you've seen her. She fell ill off the Caithness coast, and we had to put in at Kirkwall. On shore she soon recovered, and would not listen to my suggestion of crossing to Wick and taking the train south. Off the Lewis she had another attack – sea-sickness and heart trouble – and we ran for Stornoway. There Miss de Burc nursed her back to fit-ness, but it took longer this time, and I was afraid to venture to sea again. She was game, though, and persuaded me to try for Oban, where we could make rail connexion if necessary. Unfortunately we ran into a bad patch of weather. Last night we had head winds and a steep sea, and she collapsed in our hands. We put in and anchored in a sheltered bay some miles down the coast here.'

'That would be Fiskavaig,' I said.

'Probably. We were too late to do any good. My aunt never recovered from that last collapse, and died early this morn-ing. I saw by the guide-book that there was a good anchorage here, a hotel, and a motor road to Portree. So here we are, and with a good deal to do, I suppose.'

'If I can be of any assistance—'

'Thanks. We'll be glad of your help. Is this the hotel, then?'

We had arrived at the door of the little inn, and I led them into the low-ceilinged dining-room, where a smoky peat fire burned in a wide grate. We engaged a room for the lady, who, begging to be excused, left Leng and me alone to discuss ways and means. She did not look at me as she went out with the landlady, and no single word had she vouchsafed me.

'I am not too clear as to what is necessary in a situation like this,' said Leng. 'Some legal formalities are called for, no doubt.'

'I think so. There is a local constable who will know, and the distillery manager is a Justice of the Peace.'

'That should make things easy. My idea is to get my aunt's body taken to Portree, and from there conveyed by the regular carriers – boat and rail – to London. Is that feasible?'

'Quite, I should say. There is a good motor road to Portree, which is certain to have an undertaker. If we get him at the end of a wire he will do all that is necessary, and in time for the morning boat if you are anxious to catch it.'

'I am. I see my way now. Much obliged, King.'

'By the way, you'll probably need a motor for yourself and Miss de Burc.'

'I do not think so. There's the yacht. We propose to run her to Oban, where I am a member of the sailing club, and from there take the train.'

And that was that. There was little of the bereaved nephew about Edward Leng. He was cheerful and energetic, and even slightly excited. There was a fine dusky colour in his face, and his eyes had a curious trick of lighting up and dulling over as if his imagination were busy. What might be in his mind I did not let my thoughts dwell on at that time. I kept mind and body busy in promoting his arrangements, but when at last I stood alone on the landing-stage watching himself, the manager, and the constable pull off for the yacht, the wheels of my mind began to turn furiously, and drove me from that place.

I did not seek Neil Quinn. Instead, I went seaward along the shore of the loch, climbed to the brow of the green bluffs, passed through a scattered township of 'black' houses, and so reached the solitudes of unpeopled moors and braes and green, still, rushy valleys. In time I climbed a great, flat-topped, rock-ramparted hill somewhere near Talisker, and farther than that I did not go. Seated on a boss of limestone, I looked wide and far over sea and land. The sun was in the west, and the sea was a shimmering plain of gold, with the whale-back islands of Canna and Rum standing dead-black out of the shimmer. Below the high black cliffs of MacLeod's Tables stood the pinnacles of the Seven Sisters with uneasy water about their deep-planted feet, and at the horizon stretched the long, purple shadow of the Outer Isles – Uist, Barra, and Benbecula. Behind me spread the rolling, ruddy moors, pierced here and there by bold limestone bluffs, towered over by the Cuchullins, and suffused with light – austere moors, brooding, mystic, changeless, uncaring.

I stayed a long time on that hill, and when finally I turned homewards I was neither wiser nor more decided than when I came, for all the weight of musings that had come and gone. By then the sea was no longer gold but coldly blue, and the moors were solemn, hushed, lonely. It was late twilight by the time I reached the distillery house, and Quinn had the hanging lamp alight in the kitchen. He was busy at the range as I entered, and gave me a fleeting look over his shoulder.

'You have had a good long stroll,' he said casually, 'and will be needing more than your share of the chops.'

'Three will be enough for me,' I said, copying his tone.

'Good! That leaves four for me. Draw in about, then. I hope they are not over-cooked.'

They were, but we finished them notwithstanding. We spoke very little during that meal, but when we had pulled our basket-chairs to either side of the fire, and charged our pipes with the manager's Tam o' Shanter, I no longer avoided the subject that was in both our minds. The lamp was at my back, the fire was low, Quinn was gazing at the ceiling; I rested my head on my finger-tips, gazed between the bars of the grate, and began. 'What did you think of the lady, Neil?' I asked him.

Though I did not look, I knew that he was blowing smoke upwards, and running a hand through his bush of black hair.

'I do not know,' he said musingly; 'I do not know at all. She is very beautiful, of course; but what is moving behind that still face of hers I have had no chance of finding out, and it is the only thing that I want to find out.'

'Nor have I found out,' I said, and added, 'to be in the least sure.'

'I saw her again this afternoon while you were away in the hills. I was coupling on the side-car when she passed, and she gave me a smile and a nod. I suppose she guessed who I was.'

'She has heard of you. I have told her some of our less disreputable ploys together.'

'I wanted to speak to her, but she stilled her face and went by very quickly. She, to, has learned to wear a mask.'

'She has. I have seen it off for a full month, and there was something sib below. Do you know, Neil, I am strongly minded to try and save that woman against her will.'

'You mean from Leng?'

'Yes. I suppose it is from him in the first place – and from herself too.'

'You told me in Portree, yon first night, that Leng is married. I can understand that, now the aunt is dead, certain conventions are in danger of outrage. But I did not know that you were an upholder of convention. If this woman is the woman you think she is, she will not suffer wrong from any man – conventions or none.'

'One would think so. Yet there is a man waiting in Paris who, I think, would go the length of killing to save her from Leng.'

'Then there is more in this than I know.'

'There is.' And forthwith I told him much of what Murray had told me at Loch Ruighi. He listened, thinking hard, and was silent for a time after I had finished.

'That woman is a prude,' he said at last, and was again silent, and I knew so well what he meant that I made no remark. 'She is of an old and maybe pagan race, as you say,' he went on, 'and I can compare her only to Daphne, who sacrificed herself to escape pollution. This Daphne feels herself in some way smirched by Leng, and thinks that she must go to destruction with him rather than yield to a clean love. That is an extreme form of prudery.'

'I have thought all that,' I told him; 'but there is another possibility I want you to look at. She may love Leng. Why should she not? What do I and you know of women? She may even be his mistress.'

'You are leaping from extreme to extreme, as is only natural. If she does love Leng, that settles the matter. Murray, who has known her for years, thinks not, and is acting accordingly. He is out of action in Paris. Do you feel that you should take his place?'

'I did not consider the matter in that way,' I said. 'I have no use for Murray's melodrama. Frankly, I do not like interfering when I am not certain that I have anything to interfere about. And yet—'

'What would you like to do?'

'I would like to put a few things to the woman. She was with us for a month at Loch Ruighi, and proved out well according to our standard. If she is the woman we think she is—'

'I don't understand your timidity. Give the lassie credit for the best you have imagined her. You that were not much afraid of risks should not boggle at this one.'

'It is because I am not too sure of myself or of my motives, and I do not like to say the things that I have to say. But you are right, Neil. Let us help the lassie if she can be helped, and if she can't – it does not matter what we say or leave unsaid.'

I got to my feet and put my hand on Quinn's shoulder. 'Wait ye here for me,' I said. 'I will put the matter to the test this very night.'

I stalked out into the dark, and Quinn's 'Good luck' followed me.

CHAPTER XVII

I entered the lamp-lit hall of the little inn and knocked at the dining-room door.

'Come in,' said a voice; and the voice was Leng's. I was not surprised at that. I opened the door and went in. Leng was taking his ease in one of the hair-covered arm-chairs near the smouldering peat fire and smoking a long cigar. Agnes de Burc was seated on the far side of the dining-table, which was still covered by a not-too-clean tablecloth. There was a writing-pad in front of her and one or two sealed envelopes, and she held a fountain-pen in her fingers.

'Glad you called, King,' said Leng cordially. 'I was thinking of looking you up. I expect the Portree people any time now, and am waiting here for them. Pull up that chair and try one of these cigars.'

I pulled the chair round, so that I could see the two, and accepted a long corona from Leng's case. While I was scraping the blunt end of it with a fingernail the lady rose from the table. 'I will leave you two gentlemen to your smoke,' she said.

'Please do not go, Miss de Burc,' I pleaded. 'It is you I have come to see.'

Leng chuckled amiably. The lady quite calmly gathered up her correspondence. 'You really must excuse me, Mr King,' she said coldly. 'I am not in a mood for visitors, and have a good deal to do.'

This attitude was not unexpected. I rose to my feet, and she would have to pass close by me to reach the door.

'You will greatly oblige me,' I said earnestly, 'if you will stay for a few minutes. I promise that what I say will be very different from what you expect.'

That reached her. She gave me a quick look, and, for the first time, there was interest in her glance. Then she turned her eyes downwards on the white cloth, and after a little meditating pause resumed her seat. She said no word.

'Thank you,' I said, sitting down. 'I will not detain you long.'

'Perhaps I am in the way—' began Leng, making as if to rise.

'Not at all,' I said quickly. 'Please stay. What I have to say touches you too.'

'Thanks for your interest,' he said, his speculative eye on me. 'I hope you are not going to be too serious.'

I lighted my cigar, got it drawing well, made myself as comfortable as the slippery chair permitted, and turned to the lady. 'You will be thinking, young lady,' I said, 'that I am in love with you.'

Again she gave me that quick look, that look that a woman gives when she wants to know, and that so often tells her what she wants to know. My face, schooled after that long afternoon of thought, must tell her nothing. It sought only to smile at her a little playfully, a trifle mockingly, through a thin haze of smoke. Sitting upright in her chair, she placed her firm white hands on the blotting-pad in front of her, and there her eyes rested. The mask was on her face, and she waited for me to go on.

'I am not in love with you at all, my lady,' I said easily, but gently, and I went on smoking. She made no sign, but a bark of laughter came from Leng.

'You are an abrupt sort of devil,' he said with amusement. 'Where is your chivalry, man? You know, I am sorry that you are not in love.'

'I knew you would not mind, Leng,' I said. 'You are the sort of man that would treat your rivals with contempt.'

'Rivals!' he exclaimed, his eyebrows lifted. 'Had you not better be careful, Mr King?'

'Let us be frank with what we all know.'

'So you all know.' And then in a flash of anger: 'I'm damned if I care who knows – so long as Agnes does not mind. Do you want to hear any more of this silly talk, Agnes?'

'Please let Mr King finish what he has to say,' she requested.

'I fear that I gave you a false impression on the night of our misadventure on Loch Ruighi,' I went on, addressing myself to her. 'I spoke some romantic nonsense, I rather fear, but it was necessary to take strong measures to pull a gently-nurtured woman through those long hours. I believe the measures did help, and – if required, they would have been stronger.'

Still her face gave no sign, but her hands on the blotting-pad clenched and unclenched. That small sign showed how my words stung. They were meant to.

'I am glad indeed, that you do not love me,' she said in her low-pitched voice. 'But why is it necessary to tell me?'

'I will tell you that too. It is because I want you to appreciate my disinterestedness. My dear Miss de Burc, you possess great beauty and great charm, and men love you easily, or rather hardly, as Mr Leng knows. You, despite yourself, are accustomed to being loved, even importuned, and, again despite yourself, have grown accustomed to look on all men as lovers, and therefore not to be trusted as friends, since they are all selfish, desirous, and biased hopelessly. Now, so far as you are concerned, I am neither biased nor selfish nor yet desirous, and my friends judge me trustworthy. What I say to you I say as a friend only, and for the sake of friendship. Will you try and realize that?'

She inclined her head, but did not look at me. She was cold as ice, and there was no least inkling of what moved below that cold exterior. Yet I knew that a heart beat there, and that warm blood flowed there, and that somewhere far down were possibilities of passion at its highest. And also I knew that every word I uttered was surely destroying any chance I ever had of rousing that exquisite passion. But I went on nevertheless.

'Look upon me as your friend – Tom King of Loch Ruighi, hermit, wanderer, outcast in some degree, peculiar, perhaps, in his top storey. But note that I was once young, and could have loved you then as desperately as any. Do I not know that once did love? My dear, I have been through the toils, and they have left their gall on me. Once I suffered at the weak hands of a woman as bitterly as any man, and all I have done since and all I am doing now has been and is only an effort to forget – a vain effort, my lady. Now you know me.'

At that instant she gave me a blinding glance – a glance that somehow thrilled me – and again turned her eyes on her clenched hands.

'And so,' I went on evenly, 'as your hard-bitten friend, who is blinded by no sentimental mists nor has any respect for certain conventions, I tell you frankly that you are making a mistake in running away with Edward Leng.'

I heard the sudden scrape of Leng's chair on the linoleum as he rose to his feet. 'This is going too far,' he said warmly, taking a step towards me. 'Do you want to listen to this stuff, Agnes? If not, I'll soon put this fellow outside.'

Very quickly the lady turned to him. 'I will have no scene, Ted,' she said imperatively. 'Let Mr King finish. Please sit down.'

He frowned, then smiled a little grimly, and obeyed. My cigar was almost out, and I took time to get it going strongly before carrying on. I looked at the lady over the glowing end, and found her eyes on me with a new interest.

'I am glad that Mr Leng did not throw me out,' I said. 'We know how strong he is.'

'Don't be afraid,' he half sneered. 'Have you much more to say?'

I may have surprised him, but probably he was not particularly angry. He was too strong in the knowledge of his own power, and was more contemptuous than anything else.

'I am not really afraid,' I said. 'But I might be afraid if I were your rival and a possibly dangerous one.'

He shrugged his shoulders, and there was now no doubt of his contempt.

'That is the kind of man he is, my lady,' I said. 'You are his good hunting, and he'd be a dangerous man at the kill.'

'Please go on, Mr King,' she requested quietly.

'It is not easy to make clear to you what I feel so strongly. Of course, if you care for Edward Leng I am being merely impertinent, and my words will have no weight with you. That risk must be taken. I would say, then, that if you are not moved by love, you should pause here and now and consider—'

'Consider what?' questioned Leng sharply.

'Consider yourself, my dear,' I said to her. 'Consider yourself only, and not him nor me nor any other. And yet friendship is worth considering. It is a very splendid thing to have your friends think well of you. In considering them you consider yourself too. There is myself, for instance. I like you fine, my dear. Over yonder in our little testing-school by Loch Ruighi we tried you out very thoroughly, and we found that you belonged to the same stock as ourselves. You understood. It is our duty to do what we can for our own.'

'What do you think you are doing for her?' mocked Leng. 'You are only a special pleader after all, King, and I am inclined to be suspicious. I would like to probe a little into the excuse you have given for intruding with this subject. For some reason – I'm hanged if I can see how you got it – you have concluded that Miss de Burc is running away with me. No one but a peculiar devil like yourself would dare such an accusation. You must admit our tolerance. And suppose we do plead guilty, Mr King, can you give us any reason why we should not do as we please – according to your own boasted standard? And, damn it, man, does any standard at all excuse your sheer impudence?'

Leng was showing fight. He had grown heated as he went on. His black brows were drawn down, and his black eyes had a gleam in them. I chewed the end of my cigar for a little before replying.

'In my unmannerly code,' I said, 'truth justifies most statements – not all, perhaps. It is true that Miss de Burc is running away with you. It needed the driving force of friendship to make me speak to her as I am speaking. I will take all you can say about my impudence if love—'

'Don't be an ass,' he interrupted brutally. 'Would any two people run away, as we are supposed to be doing, except love – what but love would justify—?'

'Exactly,' I interrupted him in turn, and I brought my clenched hand down on the chair arm. 'If Agnes de Burc does not love you, there is nothing – nothing here or in hell – that should justify or compel her to be your mistress.'

I swung to the lady before he could speak. She sat very still, and her eyes remained downcast.

'You are young,' I told her, 'and you are lonely of spirit and you have sought no help in working out your problem. Let me help you now. I know that there is some austere spirit in you that impels you to sacrifice yourself for being once false to your ideals. Believe me, one false step never justifies another. Know you for very truth, whatever else has been preached or thought or sung, that a false step can be retraced. It can – I know it can. And, having retraced it, you will be nobler, purer, and more desirable than any austere virgin, and your lover should approach you on his knees and kiss your feet. I cannot make you see that as clearly as I can. I wish I could. If you had only a little time to consider it – a few quiet days—'

'Damn you!' cried Leng, 'I will have no more of this.'

This time his chair almost fell over backwards as he leapt to his feet. I was on my feet too. And at that instant, as if the scene had been staged, a motor-horn blared outside the inn. We paused, and, having paused, our minds became less hectic. And then, suddenly, a feeling of bleakness, weariness, utter failure came over me.

'There is your car,' I said abruptly. 'I have said all I care to say, and I'll be going. Goodnight and goodbye to ye – for I never want to see either of you again.'

119

I did not look at Agnes de Burc. I threw my dead cigar-butt amongst the smouldering peats and stalked back into the night.

CHAPTER XVIII

Neil Quinn sat staring into the kitchen fire, and his fiddle was across his knees. 'You have said your say, long man?' he said, without looking up.

'I have,' I told him, 'and the sense of failure is on me.'

'That would be so,' he half mused. 'We always went to the fight and we always fell. We fail because we aim so high, but sometimes we gain what we do not be expecting.'

'And what we do not want.'

'And that too. I will now play for you the lament that a Campbell made for the loss of Inverlochy.'

He played for me that tune, pacing slowly up and down on the stone flags – a tune of failure and defeat, and yet full of a terrible, high, unconquerable spirit: the spirit of the singer, proud of his great singing, and knowing that his song is a supreme call to the spirit of the defeated.

' 'Tis a queer race we are,' said Quinn. 'The songs we make are more important than the loss or love we sing of. "Mavrone, Mavrone, bitter was the blow," we sing. But, Christ God! what a splendid fine song we are making of it. I will now play you an old air called "To Cashel I'm Going." '

He played that tune – a fast air with a cry in it:

> 'Tis a pity I came where my name
>   Was unknown in the town,
> Where no one could tell how so well
>   I had earned renown.
> Then the young one I sought would have thought
>   Herself honoured in knowing
> A man of my name and good fame –
>   So to Cashel I'm going.

There friends I will meet in the street,
    And we'll drink the red wine
That came o'er the main out of Spain
    To cheer hearts like mine.
And no one I'll tell what a hell
    In my heart I am knowing
When I think of a face in this place –
    So to Cashel I'm going.

'That is a dance tune,' said Quinn, 'and it is a lament as
well, for the man that made it took sorrow with him in his
going. But he had a great naïve, proud spirit, and at Cashel he
was a man amongst men. We always went to the fight, says the
old word, and we always fell. But we always go, and we will
keep on going, Tom King – when it is required of us.'

My friend had the right word for me always.

CHAPTER XIX

Next day was Saturday, and, although it was my turn to wash
the dishes, I slept late, and Quinn let me sleep. When I got
down the table was already laid, the porridge-pot a-bubbling,
and the bacon sizzling in the pan. 'You will treat me as an
invalid.' I complained somewhat testily.

'You were a bit restless in your sleep,' Quinn, busy over the
tea-pot, excused himself. 'I thought a long lie would do you
no harm, and neither it would, if you got out of bed on the
right side.'

'Maybe you thought of giving me breakfast there.'

'I did, but you have saved me the trouble, and you will now
show whether you are an invalid or not. Or would you prefer a
little dry toast?'

My appetite proved my fitness, however. We talked as we
ate. 'I'm no' that ill,' I told him, 'and I slept well, though you
say I was restless.'

'You were. You muttered and twitched till the dawn.'

'Yet I had no dreams that I can remember.'

'All the better. Have no waking ones either.'

'Alas! My dreams are the "might-have-been" kind. However, let us look ahead and decide on our doings this day.'

'Know you that this is the last day of the month, and that I must render an account of my stewardship to my Lords of His Majesty's Treasury. I shall be busy with accounts all this forenoon. I know what you will be doing too.'

'Am I in such a bad way that you must order my day for me?'

'You are so. I will have no man with a grouch round my distillery. 'Tis drunk you would be getting, and me with you.'

'Surely a little of your whisky would help us to grasp the white logic of things?'

'It would. But you will grasp it in a better way by taking advantage of this unique weather for the misty isle. The loch outside is sparkling its diamonds, and there is a breeze across the heather finer than the finest usquebaugh. You will take to the moors, my father, and let the sun and the winds work on you. The Cuchullins will be watching you on the one hand, and the uncaring sea will be taking no notice of you on the other, and the cloud shadows will be racing across the hills as they have raced these eighty or eight hundred million years. All these things make for serenity – go thou and acquire it.'

'That thing I will do, O son and guide,' I said imitatively.

And so I went alone into the sunlight and the space.

At the head of the first brae I looked back at the little inn by the waterside. No one moved about it. Tufts of smoke blew from both chimneys and told me that the dining-room fire was on, from which I gathered that the lady was still a guest, since that fire was never lighted so early unless visitors were in the house. The white yacht was riding buoyantly at anchor a quarter of a mile offshore, and its tall mast and fine rigging were outlined sharply against the green braes beyond. No one moved on deck. With that one look I turned my back on inn and yacht and loch – and on more also.

I went down the long curve of Glen Brittle, with the brawling burn in the gorge below me, and the clean and silent hills towering above. At the fork of the roads I passed a little holiday camp consisting of a tent, a wagon, and an old white horse; and two young women sat at the door and peeled potatoes. 'God bless the work!' said I, but they did not answer even with a smile. Doubtless they were out of the crowded south country, and would risk nothing with the wilds and the wild men – and a wild man I might have looked. So I went on past that place whistling.

In time I came to the sea, and at the edge of the tide I stood and watched the green waves roll in and check and trip and break white on the clean shingle. How long I watched I do not know, for the unceasing march of the waves before my eyes, and the unceasing sough of the sea in my ears, put me in some kind of trance that was infinitely quiet and without thought, and yet more heavy than any weight of dreams. It was with difficulty that I shook myself free of that trance and turned to the hills behind me.

I crossed the high shoulder of Ben Breinish, came down on the deep and dark Loch Chroisg, edged round that sullen water, and faced the brae beyond. Over the head of that brae I dipped into the gentle valley of Loch Sleadale, that kindly, shallow water, with shores of sedge, where the good brown trout lurk and are not shy of the fisherman's lure. Here I encountered the farmer of Talisker on his rounds amongst his sheep and his shepherds. He was a slim, dark man, and very young to be the owner of his immense flocks, and he had given Neil Quinn and me permission to shoot and fish over his ten thousand acres. We talked for a time, and finally he said, 'Come over to my place and have some lunch.'

I noted then that I was hungry, and I went with him across three miles of moor to his high, bare, slate-house that stands unsheltered above the cliffs of Talisker, and looks out on far Mull and all the islands between. There he lived alone with an old housekeeper, who regaled us amply, and thereafter the farmer and I discussed a bottle of good port and the peculiar ways of sheep. He was master of eight thousand of these useful animals, and he knew all their ways, which are stranger ways than one would expect. We talked of breeding and crossing and acclimatizing, of percentage loss by disease, mishap, and marauding, and of percentage of profit, which was low but accumulative, of wool and the queer vagaries of its marketing, of pasturage and feeding, and of transportation and wintering on the mainland as far away as the Black Isle of Ross, which is not an island at all. He knew sheep-farming indeed, and proved to me, what I was slow to believe, that it was a most interesting, exciting, and inspiring calling.

It was well on in the evening when I set out along the lime-stone-ribbed brae for Uiskavagh, and the shadows of the lesser hills were high on the Cuchullins before I reached the distillery. Quinn was not there, nor in his office, nor in the house. The kitchen fire was out and cold, and the breakfast dishes were still on the table.

'He is on some ploy of his own,' I said. 'He deserves well at my hands, and his dinner shall be ready for him.'

I lighted the fire to a roar and examined the larder. There was in it but a little mutton, and, the blue-bottles having already found it, I threw it on the midden for all the cats that prowled. I trotted to the little general store on the brae above the distillery, and hurried back with eggs, butter, bread, bacon, and mutton, and soon I was busy and wildly inventive. I had the table laid, the lamp lighted, and a glorious odour evolved before the silence was shattered by the staccato bark of Quinn's Rudge on the road outside. He came in stamping his feet, slapping his hands, and sniffing with ardour.

'Good!' he cried; 'and then better! 'Tis grand cooking that's in it this blessed night for a famished man. There is a nip coming in the evening air, and I forgot my overalls.'

'Been trying out the old crock?' I inquired, my hand on the handle of the frying-pan. 'She petered out on a hill somewhere, of course?'

'She did not. Never was there a machine like that one. She went roaring up the hill of – she went roaring up every hill. I couldn't hold her, and went farther than I thought I would go when you left here this morning. What kind of day did you have?'

'I had a good day. The Cuchullins watched me patiently on the one hand; the sea spoke to me on the other, for all that it did not care; the moors cradled me; the wind blew through me; I raced the cloud shadows; and the farmer of Talisker

124

nourished me with food and wine. I had a good day, and I will have many better. Come now and be fed.'

Quinn was in very high fettle. His eyes sparkled, and his ironic Irish face was twisted by some inward and joyous spirit that now made him laugh to himself, and again drove him to speech, whether his mouth was full or empty. 'This has been a great day,' he said time and again. 'I did enjoy this fine day. You should have enjoyed it too.'

'Did I not say so?'

'But you should have enjoyed it as it deserved, and that you did not do. Enjoyment is summed up in the contemplation of one's own prowess. Did you contemplate your own prowess?'

'Prowess in what, you silly ass?'

'In lots of things. A man can do most things in his own mind.'

'I know what I cannot do, anyway.'

'Maybe you do. Maybe you do,' agreed Quinn cheerfully.

We had removed the dishes to the scullery sink and were seated in our basket-chairs before the fire smoking a first pipe when a loud knocking came at the front door, and footsteps tramped down the long passage towards us. We turned our heads to the closed door and wondered who came. Someone fumbled for the handle, and 'Come in!' cried Quinn. The door opened, and Edward Leng stood looking in at us.

CHAPTER XX

Edward Leng stood in the doorway, his bare, sleek head almost reaching the lintel, and his great shoulders filling the frame. There was a high colour on his face, and his brows were drawn down. 'Excuse me interrupting,' he said shortly. 'Have you fellows seen Miss de Burc this afternoon?'

The question startled me, and brought me to my feet. 'Is she not at the inn?' I questioned in turn.

'She is not, nor is she on board the yacht. Have you seen her?'

Quinn replied for me. He was reclining comfortably in his

chair and smoking industriously. 'He has not,' he said quickly but carelessly. 'And he would not tell you if he had seen her.'

That rather uncalled-for reply kept me silent, and it did not hasten Leng's speech. He glared at Quinn for a moment, and then turned to me, his frown more marked. 'I half expected this attitude,' he said, forcing his voice to be calm, 'and I will not be roused by it just yet. I am going back to the inn to see if she has returned within the last half-hour; but, if she has not, you will have me back here immediately.'

There was an unmistakable threat in his last words. He turned at once and went stamping down the hall, and I remained on my feet, gazing stupidly at the empty doorway.

'Did you hear him, Neil?' I asked.

'I heard him say that he was coming back,' said Neil lightly. 'Shall we lock our doors against the dangerous man?'

'But about Agnes de Burc? Some mishap—'

'Sit down,' said he. 'That woman, I am thinking, will be able to take care of herself, wherever she is.'

'Where would she be at this hour unless—'

'How could I be knowing where she is *now*?' he said. 'She might have as much reason as another for taking to the moors on a day like this.'

'She may be lost, man.'

'She is not lost. I know that much, anyway.'

'What do you know, Quinn?' I probably showed some excitement. 'Tell me,' I asked quickly, 'has she gone away?'

'She has gone away. Hush! here comes Leng. I will tell you, if I must, later on.'

I sat down hurriedly. 'I hope the man will do nothing foolish,' I said.

'He will do that. Remember you know nothing, and do not stand any of his bullying.'

Leng came in – without knocking this time. He strode straight down the passage and in at the door, which he shut behind him. He placed his back against the panels and concentrated on me entirely. 'Miss de Burc is not at the inn,' he said, strangely calm.

'I am glad of that,' I said, equally calm. I had regained some poise, and looked at the man curiously. He was no longer flushed and hot, but pale and composed. Never before had I seen this pallor on his face, and it more than ever emphasized the ancient Eastern type of the man; the high sloping forehead, black bar of brow, unreadable eyes, high nose, moulded lips, heavy jaw – these with the high, wide shoulders and lean hips reminded me more than ever of the old carvings of the Assyrians. Knowing something of the great and dark records of that people, I wondered what he might be capable of.

'Let us have no scene,' he said reasonably. 'I ask nothing of you lightly, and I will tell you all I know first. I left Miss de Burc at the inn last night, and went to Portree. It was late in the afternoon when I got back – we broke a wheel near a place called Sligachan – and she was not at the inn then, nor was she on the yacht. I was not anxious, however, for she is fond of wild country, as you know, and might be out on the moors. But as time elapsed and she did not return I started to make inquiries. The landlady told me that she saw Miss de Burc going towards the distillery at about ten in the morning, and had not seen her since. On examining her room we found that her bag – a small one – was gone too, and that made me remember the talk you treated her to last night. That is why I am here. You see I am frank with you, King. I put it to you that either you know where she has gone, or you are taking her disappearance and her danger with a callousness that you have not shown hitherto where she is concerned.'

He stopped there, his eyes on me searchingly, and at once I replied. 'I do not know where Miss de Burc is,' I said.

'How am I to believe you?' he gave back, still calmly. 'I cannot trust you or your breed. About this fellow here you once equivocated to me. Are you doing that now? You do not know where she is, you say, but I think you know why she went, and her destination.'

'You are right not to trust me,' I told him, 'because I would not tell you anything, even if I knew. Sooner than help you to find Agnes de Burc, I would lie most convincingly to the detriment of my soul. To prevent you finding her I would go to great lengths, Mr Leng – say to the length of trying to break you in two with my bare hands. Is that a frankness equal to your own?'

'Now we have your true colours,' he said grimly, and strode across towards me. I rose to meet him, and we stood face to face, eyes level.

'King,' he said, his teeth bare below moulded lips, 'you know where my woman is, and I will have that knowledge out of you.'

He caught me by the shoulder, and I called to mind how, on a day by the Leonach, having caught Ncil Quinn thus, he had next instant measured his length on the gravel. But I had no intention of acting thus – for yet awhile, at any rate – and so kept my arms hanging loosely at my side, loose but ready. Still, a little tingle flashed through me and blinded me for the fraction of a second, and it is possible that my forbearance would not have stood much of strain had not Quinn spoken from his chair at Leng's back.

'I am the man you should be man-handling, bully man,' said he. 'I took Miss de Burc away on my motor-cycle, and she is now safely beyond your reach.'

Like a flash Leng turned, his arm aswing, and his open palm caught Quinn a resounding smack on the cheek, and knocked him clean off his chair. 'That is for you, you young cub!' he growled.

Thereafter, Quinn's quickness surprised him, and surprised me. Even as he fell he twisted, so that his first contact with the floor was purchase for the leap he made. I was altogether too slow to act. Leng had barely spoken before Quinn's leap sent him staggering back, and as he staggered he took two quick blows on the mouth. Such active ferocity I never imagined in that lad, or in any lad. He was actually explosive, and it kept on exploding. His blows rained in from all angles on body, shoulders, and head, and for the moment Leng was over-whelmed. But only for the moment. With a boxer's skill he pulled himself together, thrust down Quinn's arms, and countered him with a left-hand clip to the head. The blow was too high to be deadly, but it knocked the lad off his feet.

And here again Quinn showed his quickness, for his touch on the floor was, Antæus-like, the starting-point of a swing that caught Leng under the jaw, and staggered him into the corner by the table.

Leng, using his weight, bored out to mid-floor, and after a fierce rally again got in that left-arm blow. As Quinn swayed, Leng, judging his distance, uppercut with his right. I heard the crisp click of the blow, and poor Quinn toppled forward on his knees, fell sideways, and rolled over on his back.

I suppose I should have interfered long before this. I wanted to, but Quinn's fury and speed so astonished me – and perhaps also so pleased – that I could not make up my mind in time. The lad was on his back and out before I could decide.

Leng stood swaying over Quinn, and I sprang forward and thrust him back to the dresser. I twisted a long basket-chair half round, and lifted Quinn on it. He came to almost immediately, and before I could move towards the sink for some cold water. I held him down in the chair, though he struggled under my hands.

'I'm only just beginning,' he protested. 'I can fight all night.'

'You have been on your back a full minute,' I lied to him. 'A clean knock-out, my son, and nothing more to be said. Look at our friend yonder. You have knocked the fight out of him, at any rate.'

And that was so. Leng, for some reason, was as nearly winded as a man could be and retain his feet. He leant aside on the table, his head down and his breath coming in gasps. Presently he blindly pulled the other basket-chair towards him, and fell into it, his head over the arm-rest, and his nose dripping blood on the stone floor. His heart seemed to have played out on him, and his struggle for breath frightened me.

'He'll collapse in our hands,' I cried. 'Sit you still, Neil. You are not fit to move yet.'

I jumped into the scullery, plucked a towel off the line, damped it under the cold tap, hurried to Leng's side, and bathed his neck and face. The cold water helped him wonderfully. He threw himself back in the chair and his breath came easier.

'Keep that towel to your nose,' I said brusquely. 'You'll be all right in a minute.'

Next I used a drying-cloth on Quinn's face, which was scarcely marked. There was a darkish flush on brow and temple, and a graze on his chin oozed a little blood. That was all. As I wiped his face solicitously, he suddenly burst into laughter.

'Don't be an old fool, Tom,' he said. 'I'm all right. My head buzzes a bit, but a mouthful of Uiskavagh would settle that.'

'Of course,' I cried. 'I forgot that whisky. Both of you are needing some.'

I went to the wall-cupboard by the fireplace and poured two stiff drams of neat spirit. Leng tossed his off, grimaced, and sat up. His nose had stopped bleeding, but a little trickle still oozed from a gash in his lip. I stood looking down on him, the empty glass in my hand, and he put his hands on the arm-rests of the chair as if about to rise.

'Do not hurry,' I told him. 'All fighting is over for the night, and much good it has done you. You are not in any form to give me what you think is due.'

He said nothing to that – the fighting spirit was entirely departed.

'There is no use talking to you,' I went on, 'and it would look like taking advantage of you as you are now. As soon as you are rested we shall be glad to see the last of you – the very last of you, remember, Mr Leng. That is all I will say.'

I stepped back to the fireplace, and Leng, without a word, rose to his feet. As he turned he staggered a little, and stepped out with a sort of drunken steadiness that showed he was far from recovered.

'I will see you to your boat,' I told him, 'so that this incident may finish harmlessly. You stay where you are, Neil – I shan't be a minute.'

Leng neither by word nor gesture objected to my company. I preceded him down the dark passage, where I opened the door, and assisted him down the steps and along the path to the road. There we walked side by side towards the distillery and the landing-stage. It was a dark night, but not dead black. The grey road glimmered in front; the great sweeps of hill stood out black and still against a frosty splendour of stars; and the riding-light of the yacht laid down a narrow path of brilliance on the water. There was no least sound out of earth or sea or sky. As we passed the end of the lane leading to the inn Leng halted abruptly and turned towards it. 'She is not there. She is not there,' he said in a grieved tone, the tone of a man who has lost his poise. He faced me and caught my arm. 'I cannot find her, King,' he said, 'and I must find her.'

I could not see his face, but could not help knowing that the man had broken down, softened, deliquesced in some strange fashion.

'You can have no help from me,' I told him.

'I know that,' he agreed, in the same low voice. 'I know that now. You will tell me nothing, no matter what I do or try. And you know what I so much want to know. That is beastly. For look you, King, that woman is mine, yet I cannot possess her. For five years I have known her, and she is different from other women. That I know, who have known many women. They were no mates of mine. Life has been too easy to me. What I have reached my hand for has not been denied me – except this one woman, who is a fit mate for any man, and full of rich passion, could I only move it. And I had so nearly moved it. Damn you, King! Damn— But I must not think of what I owe you – I that have always paid my debts fully.'

His hand shook on my arm and some fervour had awaked in his voice.

'You are surely paying your debts now,' I said grimly; 'and they are debts you did not think to pay, you lascivious dog! Come on, and get aboard your yacht.'

I shook his hand away roughly and strode down the road. He followed without a word, and without a word he got into the dinghy by the landing-stage. 'Go on, damn you!' he said to the sailor who still held on to the planks, and he passed out of my life – as I thought – into the night. No word more of hate or valediction passed between us: the only sound was the dip of the oars gradually dying.

CHAPTER XXI

I did not stay long by the shore. For one thing, the island midges found me pipeless; and for another, Quinn was back at the house burdened with a tale I was anxious to hear. I found him sitting forward in his chair and rubbing the back of his neck. He lifted his head as I came in, and grinned at me ruefully.

'Did you drown him?' he asked.

'I did not. He is dead enough. How are you feeling yourself?'

'Fit as ever,' he said, 'only for a small discomfort – not really an ache – at the back of my neck. Dash it all, Tom, I should have licked him.'

'You very nearly did. If you had escaped that uppercut and got in another rally we should be still bringing him round.'

'I don't know. You have no idea how strong he is. Still, it was a hot thing while it lasted. You are not very angry, are you?'

'Only with myself for letting you bear the brunt. His spite was set on me until you drew it on yourself – and by the way—'

'I wonder if he could lick you too?' interrupted Quinn speculatively.

'Very likely. I am not as young as I once was. But don't think you'll evade me, my son. Come on, then, and make a clean breast of it. What have you been doing during the past twelve hours?'

'Do you think a promise is binding?'

'It is – you promised me—'

'But I promised a certain lady to keep her secret for twenty-four hours.'

'Oh, very well—'

'Still, as I have already broken my promise – and got a broken head in exchange – I may as well make a clean breast of it. I can do no harm by telling you. Man, I have been on tenterhooks all the evening just to give you a hint or so. It was the finest thing that ever was on land or sea. Pour out another small drink – I might need it.'

He chuckled, and pulled his chair over to me. I was a little excited myself.

'This morning,' he began, 'shortly after you had gone into the hills, I proceeded unwillingly to the office to do some of the work for which a trusting Department pays me so lavishly – alack! I was into my accounting and had not seen anyone pass the window. My first intimation of a visitor was a small knocking at the door, and "Come in!" I yelped, wondering who the very polite person could be amongst the scoundrels of Skye, where no one knocks at a door. "Come in! hang you!" and in came my lady – as you call her – and at once drained all the old thoughts out of my mind and set new ones running. She did so, Tom King, and be damned to you! I lost my fine manners for a bit, and gaped at her, till she bid me a "Good morning, Mr Quinn." No, she would not sit down. She would not detain me a minute. She came across to the other side of the high double desk, and gave me that direct look of hers.

' "I want – your advice, Mr Quinn," she said very quietly; but, having said that much, she hesitated, as if she found it difficult to go on. I was at least surprised, and gratified too, of course, for it is not often that anyone, far less a young and beautiful woman, seeks the advice I am always ready to give. I was so surprised that I forgot to put on the solemn air of wisdom, and the lady was again speaking before I remembered. She was picking her words with some difficulty, but her eyes never wavered.

' "Mr King has told me a good deal about you, Mr Quinn," she said.

' "You should not be heeding half the things he might be saying about me," I protested. 'He has no room to speak, anyway."

'That drew a small smile, and made things easier for her. She tackled the heart of her affair at once.

' "I want to leave the island," she said boldly, "and at once – I want to leave it today. Can you advise me how I am to do it?" She was as direct as that.

'Look you, now, as soon as she had said that, I knew exactly what we were going to do. But I was not hasty. Instead, I considered with knitted brow, and produced: "The mail-boat left Portree at seven this morning, and there will not be another till Monday – tomorrow being Sunday. Now, there's Broadford, where the boat calls – but you could never get there in time. The only chance is to make Kyleakin opposite Lochalsh, which is the rail terminus—"

'"Can I make it?" She was eager.

'"You would need a car, and a fastish one," I told her, "and the nearest one is at Portree. Still, if you were wanting to go urgently—"

'"I do want to go urgently," she said; and then in a burst of confidence: "My position here is a very difficult one, Mr Quinn, and I must get away from it – quietly if I can – but I must get away at all costs."

'And at that I came round to her side of the desk.

' "My dear young lady," I said, "I am your friend, because you are the friend of my friend, and I am the only man in the island who can get you to the Kyle in time. Have you any luggage?"

'"Only a small bag."

'"Good! listen now. Go straight back to the inn and get your bag ready. Stay in your room until you hear the bark of a motor-cycle at the head of the lane, and stay there yet awhile till you hear me stump into the kitchen and start a gossip with the worthy Mrs Macdonal'. Then slip out as quickly as you may, drop your bag in the side-car of the motor-cycle at the lane-head, and proceed up the road until you reach the dip where the burn crosses. Wait there for me."

'"Oh! but, my friend," she said close to me, "I am asking too much of you."

'"You are not asking anything of me, my lady," I said. "But you must hurry now, for our time is short."

'So it was, but also I hurried her because her lip trembled, and there was a little glisten in her eyes. Slight the tremor and little the moisture, but myself I wanted to cry somehow. That is the kind of woman she is.'

'You know her,' I said. 'Go on!'

'Well, we did exactly as I had planned, and no one saw us go. My trusty steed seemed to know what was expected of her, and never coughed a protest. She took the hills in her stride, and the valleys roared behind us. No bike ever went up Dearg Ard – Applecross Brae is nothing to it – as she went up. The road is mostly loose gravel between the bumps, and I was grateful for the bumps because the back wheel would not bite the gravel. We got to the top in one rush, my passenger hanging on to the side-car with one hand and to her hat with the other. There was a keen and joyful light in her eyes, and she smiled at me bravely when I had time to look – which was not as often as I would have liked, and be damned to you again, Thomas King! From the head of the brae above Broadford I could see all the sound down to Kyle, and there was the old *Glencoe* a bare mile out from Lochalsh and the motor ferry-boat halfway across to Kyleakin. It was then that I opened out the throttle, and we did that last eight miles of twisty road in something under the quarter. All the same, we missed the ferry, which was halfway over to Lochalsh when we reached the jetty.'

He paused, and laughed at some happy thought of his own.

'But you got over all right,' I said.

'So we did. We borrowed a small boat by piracy. There was a middle-aged fisherman a little way up the beach coiling lines on the stern-board of a small coble. Him we approached with a request to put us across.

' "She will be too rough, whatever," he said; and certainly there was a nasty bit of tide-rip facing us.

' "Hire her to me, then," I urged him. "We must catch the mail."

' "She will not, then," he refused. "The bit boat might be lost on me."

'And from that he would not budge, but then I had no time to use all my pacific persuasions. Moreover, he was a small man, and he conveniently turned his back to me, and, before he could express more than one or two strangled comments, I had given him the peeler's march a matter of fifty yards up the beach.

'When he got back we were afloat, and I poked him off with an oar. He forgot all his English in remonstrating, and it was as well that the lady did not know the Gaelic, for he insisted that I was the son and grandson as well of an un-named and infinitely misbegotten female dog, and that the woman – who was laughing – was a doubly-begotten sister of the same disgraceful hound, and, moreover, that himself and his son and all the clan of the MacRonalds would be putting their black knives into my belly that day, and next day, and every day for two weeks.

'We got over without wetting the gunwale. It is a bare half-mile, and I put all I knew into the work. When we got within shouting distance of the pier I yelled to the harbour-master to hold the train for us. He trotted off to do that, for he is all of a good man and an able judge of Uiskavagh. So everything was splendid. It is not everyone the mail waits for, and all the passengers were staring at us as we went up the platform, and they, everyone, saw her take that hand – look at it! – in both of hers.'

' "When you and your friends take a thing in hand, Neil – Mr Quinn," she said, just like that, "you do that thing always."

' "We like doing things for our friends, ma'am," said I.

' "I owe much to you and your friends," said she, "and all I ask of you now is that you will not tell anyone – anyone – that I am gone – until tomorrow."

' "I will not tell anyone ever, if you wish, my lady," said I.

' "Only till tomorrow," she said. "I want that start."

'That, I felt, was meant for Leng. And at the end she leant out of the carriage window and put me a question: "How long is your friend to be with you?"

'And I told her for another fortnight.

' "Then tell him," she requested, "that before that time elapses I shall write him my thanks and my farewell."

'Mark you that – her thanks and her farewell. And I could not ask her "why farewell?" because the train moved off, and left me standing on the platform and feeling sort of empty and forlorn. And was not that a queer feeling?'

'It was. You will never see her again, and neither shall I.'

'And why not, in the name of God?'

'Because last night I told her that I never wanted to see her again.'

136

'Thunder! Why in glory did you make such an ass of your-self?'

I told him then all that had taken place at the inn on the previous evening, and at the end he said only half resignedly: 'Well, well! Maybe better you could not be doing at that time, when much had to be done in the dark. Still and all, I will be considering the future with a certain hope.'

'Don't be troubling yourself. The great thing is that we have given the woman a fresh outlook.'

'And baffled Leng, as was past needing. I failed to give him the rest of his desserts tonight, but maybe he deserves a little consolation for all he has lost. It is hard to blame him, mind you.'

'I never blamed him. You did not give him much consolation either. But let be. How did you get away from the angry MacRonalds, who are a proud and touchy people?'

'I know that. When I came down to the pier I could see that my fisherman over the water had gathered his tail behind him and impounded the Rudge. Said I to the station-agent: "Yonder is the only place in Skye where a bloody battle has not been fought, but one will be fought there this day, God help me!" And I told him of my piracy. He laughed like the old war-horse that he is, and: "We'll gather a tail of our own," says he. So we did: the harbour-master, the mate of the *Glencoe*, and at the hotel, where we went to acquire courage, we enlisted Jack Fletcher, the officer of Loch Carron, and his preventive-man. We went across in the ferry-boat, towing the coble – but Kyleakin is still without its bloody battle. The islanders, seeing the array I led, thought it prudent to parley before the onfall, and we made an honourable peace with the aid of a pound-note and a bottomless flask that was in the lock-up of the side-car. So here I am, skin-whole, with my bloody battle behind me, and a stiff neck to remember it by.'

'It is time you were in bed, then,' I ordered; and to bed we went.

But sleep held off from me for a long time, for I had much to think about, and but little satisfaction in the thinking.

CHAPTER XXII

Sunday gave us a sample of real Skye weather – a west wind and a driving wet mist. The Cuchullins and all the welter of red hills were hidden below a thick grey pall, and hurrying, wrinkled, choppy little waves ran over the bluish-grey surface of the loch.

Quinn and I spent a lazy day. After a late breakfast we stood for a while at the front door and watched the mist squalls drive up the loch, and the white yacht kick at her anchor. We speculated on the mental and physical state of her owner. The dinghy had been lifted inboard, and no one moved on the deck; it was unlikely that anyone would risk coming ashore while that weather lasted. Yet, bad though the weather was, the island folk did not shirk going to church; we saw them – small black figures – moving on all the wayward paths that led to the bare and wind-beaten little edifice at the head of a brae. Some who passed as we stood at the door looked at us with a severe and disapproving eye, for we were outlanders, and likely to be Auld Kirkers or even Papists.

'Would you like to listen to a two-hour sermon compounded of righteousness and hell-fire?' asked Quinn.

'Do I need such drastic treatment?'

'You do. The religion these people really need is some mild and genial form of Catholicity.'

'The Papistry is speaking out of your mouth.'

'You know the kind of Papist I am! You will admit that a man has to be helped against his physical surroundings as well as against his moral inside, and that the physical surroundings here make for a certain gloomy quality of mind that needs a solace, and is yet accentuated by the religion preached up yonder.'

'Has Calvinism, then, helped to sadden and narrow the race? Can you prove it?'

'The old records and the old tales prove it, I think. In the old days the islanders took life easily, and there was no hurry in their goings or in their returnings. There is a ford over in Uist, and there used to be a hostelry on the south side of it, where the piping was never done, and the old songs were at the singing weekday and Sunday. A man hurrying across the ford, or hurrying to cross it at low water, would look in for a hasty bite and sup, and be intrigued with the turn of a tune. He might stay a day, or he might stay a week, but at his going the host would say to him: "Man, man! Are you on top of the road already? Isn't it the great pity that it is not coming you are instead of going?"'

'There seems to be some change nowadays.'

'And yet the people, keen-minded as they naturally are, and obsessed by their surroundings, are merely carrying Calvinism to its logical conclusion, and have arrived at their present rigid form of election and damnation same as the Jansenists.'

'There speaks the Irishman who takes his own God lightly.'

'But consider the spiritual evolution of a youth bred in this land of rocks, heather, and stormy seas, and for ever listening to prayers and preachings of doom and hell's fire.'

We considered in our minds for a space, and out of that speculation I presently asked him: 'What, then, must they think of us?'

'Oh, we are so certainly damned that they tolerate us for the little time given us before we burn. And some of them envy us.'

'I think I follow you. If your theory is sound, which it is not, salvation, even for the most righteous amongst these people, will become so difficult that they will despair of winning it. That means foredoomed negation.'

'And worse. They will sin secretly and shamelessly, knowing that damnation is inevitable.'

'Their only hope, then, is the abolition of religion and the promotion of an intellectual rationalism?'

'Being what I am, I hold that a genial Catholicity would serve – a hopeful sort of faith, encouraging light-heartedness, gaiety, even fun.'

'You would need a modern Columba.'

'You would need Christ himself,' said Quinn; and, so rounding off that subject, we returned to our cosy kitchen, there to smoke and dispute endlessly, and flavour a little twenty-year-old Uiskavagh.

CHAPTER XXIII

We saw nothing of Leng all that Sunday. No one came ashore off the yacht, and, of course, no self-respecting islander would dream of going on the water on the Sabbath. The little vessel had the whole tumbled loch to herself, and gave no evidence of life.

But on Monday we saw something of our man, and followed his movements with some interest.

The wind had died down by then, but the rain fell steadily all day, and confined us to the house or to the distillery office. We were in the latter, and I was idly engaged in a pencil caricature of Quinn, when footsteps on the cobbles outside made me look up in time to see Leng pass the window. Neil strolled to the door and gazed after him.

'What a strapping figure he cuts in his oilskins!' he said. 'I was a cheeky young devil to try a fall out of him. He is in to the post-office up the road. He'll be needing a stamp, or a box of matches – or maybe he'll be sending a wire.'

'Whom would he be wiring anyway?' I asked idly.

'I can find out, if you want to know.'

'No! That man is not troubling me any more.'

'Maybe not, but he may be troubling your lady.'

'My lady! She is her own woman now.'

'All the same, Mr Leng is not the man to accept defeat so easily. It is not his way. I would not be surprised if, at this moment, he was trying to get the lady at the end of a wire. Probably he has worked out some scheme, and is putting it to the test before lifting sail. Why else did he not take advantage of yesterday's breeze and get out to sea?'

'Something in that,' I admitted with some discomfort.

'I wonder where she is gone, that lady,' mused Quinn.

'South, and far, I hope—' And then another thought struck me, and I added in a voice he could not catch, 'There is a place that she might go to, and yet I am thinking she would not go there now. She would be safe in that place too, and she would not be lonely, either.'

'*Om mani pudme hum*,' mumbled Quinn from the doorway. 'Is it a rosary you are saying? Here comes Leng.'

Quinn leant against the door-post, and Leng stalked by without turning his head.

'Not a word or a glance,' grinned Quinn, coming back to his desk. 'He is no' friends wi' me the day, though my marks are on him – he has a bit sticking-plaster below his lip, and a nose, and half a nose besides. Favours received are soon forgotten.'

My mind was dallying with a queer notion, and it would keep dallying with it as the hours went by. It made me take an interest in Leng's movements, and so restricted my own. After an early lunch I manoeuvred Quinn back to the distillery office, and, as the rain still fell steadily, he did not propose to go farther afield. We were in the manager's office, across the passage from Quinn's, talking shop, which is whisky and the peculiar activities surrounding it, when the old postmaster opened the door – without knocking, of course – and thrust in his head. 'I have a telegram for Mr Leng out yonder,' he said to the manager. 'Can I be borrowing your coble for a minute, Mr Grigor?'

'Shairly, Dhonal, shairly,' said the manager, an honest Aberdonian. 'Come awa' ben an' ha'e something to keep the cauld weet oot.'

'I will that,' said Dhonal readily. 'Thank you, manager. That will be enough now. No water for me. *Slainte*, gentlemen! The rain will be taking off before long, I am thinking.'

Quinn, who had been looking at the loch through the rear window, here spoke. 'You'll not be needing the coble, Dhonal. Your man is coming off in the dinghy.'

'Good, then!' cried Dhonal, throwing off the last of his dram. 'I will be going down to meet him.'

In a little while Leng and the postmaster passed the window.

'He is for sending another wire,' said Quinn to me.

'He might be,' I admitted, and my queer notion still with me, I added, 'I wouldn't be surprised if Leng took his departure before night.'

'Good sailing weather, all right,' agreed Quinn. But I knew that if Leng departed he would not go by sea.

After that we talked desultorily, and drank a little of the wonderful whisky, until, the rain clearing off, as the post-master had foretold, Quinn and I set off on a vigorous tramp. We kept to the Portree road, for the moor and the winding paths were soaking wet. There was a sound of running water everywhere, and the moors were ruddy and glistening beneath the sun-rays streaming level through the cloud portals of the west. Great fleecy bands of pearl-white mist circled the Cuchullins and bridged every glen and corrie, and the sheer pinnacles lifted into a washed sky of wonderful green and shone with red and pink and saffron-orange.

Some distance beyond the bridge across the now angry burn we met a hurrying motor. It was a Ford hackney, and contained only the driver.

'That car,' I said, 'is the answer to Leng's last wire.'

'By gosh! I believe you're right. He is not going by his yacht, then, but by the morning boat from Portree. He must be in a hurry. Blast him for an obstinate dog! I have no use for a man that will not take his beating gallantly.'

'He is doing a foolish thing, I think,' I said; and to myself I added, 'and a dangerous thing if he is going where I think he is going.'

''Tis a pity,' said Quinn wistfully, 'that someone would not wallop some decency into him.'

'Maybe a wallop or two is coming to him,' I agreed.

Before we had gone another mile the car overtook us. We stepped into the heather off the narrow road to let it go by. Leng sat beside the driver and, with head set stiffly forward, ignored us.

'You were right,' said Quinn. 'That's an end of the portent.'

When in the gloaming we got back to the distillery we at once saw that the yacht was no longer at its anchorage, and not a wing of it was visible down the reaches of the loch.

'A complete riddance,' said Quinn, 'and a sweeter, easier feel in the air. We can now resume living. Tomorrow the trout will be greedy in Sleadale and the grouse lie close in the heather.'

Yet I did not feel that easiness in the air, nor did I contemplate with any pleasure a day in the hills. I was restless, yet un-argumentative, and Neil soon noticed my mood and, adjudging its cause, treated me leniently. While it was still early he manifested sleepiness and suggested bed.

I did not sleep well that night. There was a weight on my mind that I could not account for, something tugging at my subconscious self that was outside reason. The weariness and the sense of loss I could well understand, but beyond these there was some psychic force all about me that I could not, or would not, interpret. All night long in the snatches of unquiet sleep I was made sorrowful by the face of Agnes de Burc. It was no longer the still face I knew, but a troubled, agonized, somehow pitifully innocent face, with an appeal in it that evaded me. And her eyes were hidden from me until I fell into the heavy sleep that comes at the dawn, and in that sleep her face with all its sombre and troubling beauty came close to mine, and her dark eyes looked into mine with such a look of tragedy that I started wide awake and trembling. In the very last moment before waking I had indescribable sense of woe, doom, inevitability, that sometimes comes to a man in a nightmare of eternity. I found myself sitting up in bed, and already my mind was made up. I knew exactly what I had to do, and with that knowledge came a sudden feeling of serenity that completely swept away the weight of gloom that had oppressed me.

My sitting up in bed wakened Neil Quinn.

'What is it, Tom?' he asked. 'Can't you sleep?'

'It is the dawn,' said I. 'I can see the lifeless tone of it on the water.'

'It is a thing I never cared to see,' said Quinn. 'Every dawn is hopeless, and forlorn, and inhuman, and the good God meant us to sleep till wakened by the sun.'

'You will not sleep,' I told him, 'until you have heard what is in my mind.'

I told him simply and fully.

'My guess may be entirely out,' I said at the end, 'but I am driven to do what I intend doing this day.'

'That is the thing you must do,' said my friend.

'I don't quite know why, either.'

'That will be seen in time. What concerns us now is to get the old Rudge on the road for another long run.'

'There is no hurry. You'll be able to finish your sleep.'

'No more sleep for me. I have had a fine long sleep anyway, and that is more than you can say. The road before us is a long road and a bad road, and we'll allow a good margin for accidents, and, moreover, you must get across the ferry before the old *Glencoe* waddles down the sound.'

And the dawn was no longer hopeless.

CHAPTER XXIV

I said goodbye to Neil Quinn at the Kyleakin side of the ferry, after a non-stop run down the long island between the Cuchullins and the sea.

'I am sorry to be leaving you,' I said.

'And I am sorry you are going – and yet I am not. This adventure is not yet finished, and what the finish will be I do not know, but can guess. In a fortnight I will be up to see you at Loch Ruighi – if you are there.'

'I will be there. If you can get some leave, you and I might take a small jaunt to the Spain of our dreams.'

'We will do that some day, but it may not be this October. Here comes the ferry-boat. See that you make a clean finish this time.'

The pier at the Kyle of Lochalsh is but a continuation of the railway platform, and from behind a pillar I watched the tubby *Glencoe* bucket down the sound. While she was yet a hundred fathoms off the shore I made out the tall figure of Edward Leng on the upper-deck, and, waiting to see no more, slipped up the platform on the offside of the waiting train. I took a seat in the third-class compartment next the tender, knowing that Leng would travel first, farther back. I had that jolty compartment all to myself right across the watershed to Dingwall, on the other side of Scotland. There we changed to the main line for Inverness, and as the train was waiting for us at the other side of the platform I at once slipped across through the crowd to the carriage opposite. Leng I did not pause to look for.

At Inverness, for some reason of transit convenience, the engine does not lead the train into the station, but, instead, slants off at an angle, and then pushes the coaches back to the main platform. This suited me perfectly, for it meant that I alighted at the end farthest from the entrance barrier, and so could follow Leng without much chance of being seen by him. I made out his big shoulders above the crowd, and kept him in view as he forged through the press. He made directly for the entrance barrier and disappeared. This puzzled me, for the east-bound train, which I expected him to take, was already blowing off steam at a nearby platform. I hurried to the barrier, and, having got there, as hurriedly started back out of sight. For in the station-yard, within a dozen yards of me, stood Leng speaking to a white-capped chauffeur, who held open the door of a grey touring car. It was the same car that Leng had used at Reroppe, and the last time I had seen the white-capped chauffeur he was writhing under the harsh knee of Neil Quinn.

This was a development I had not expected, and yet I might have. Leng and Agnes de Burc had come to Inverness by motor to embark on that ill-fated cruise, and it was only natural that he should use the same mode of conveyance on the return journey. I stood well back out of sight, pulling my nose and considering probabilities.

'Let me see, now,' I mused. 'Forty miles by rail and a tramp of six across the moor – that's my part of the circle. He on the other curve is faced by fifty miles of collar-work across the hills. It should be a near thing, and we may yet meet where he is not expecting to meet *me*.'

Here I took another peep through the barrier. The car and the chauffeur were still there, but Leng was not.

'He'll be in the Station Hotel for a meal,' I decided, 'and that is a thing I am needing myself. I'll have time to snatch a bite or two at Forres.'

So I took the east-bound train along the Moray coast, and got off at Forres to join the south-going train across the Grampians. At Forres I had a scheduled wait of twenty minutes, and had a hurried meal. I need not have hurried. It was market-day, and the little local train, waiting, after its easy-going fashion, until it had gathered its full complement of more or less sober farmers and crofters, was half an hour late when finally it pulled out on its uphill journey. Immediately out of Forres the line begins to rise, and keeps on rising through pine-woods and bleak grey fields until at last it comes out on the great open sweeps of moor that I knew and loved. At Barnagh, a thousand feet above sea-level, I was amongst my own quiet hills.

There I was finally done with railway travelling, and as I stepped on the platform a lucky inspiration came to me. The station-master, who was also postmaster, was an acquaintance of long standing, and I had no difficulty in borrowing one of His Majesty's red-painted service bicycles. Mounted on this, I made good time over the six miles of sandy road that mean-dered through the hills. The sun had already set before I left the station, and, as ever, the wonderful quietude of the moor-land gloaming touched the deep-down places in me. Though I had suffered and was then suffering from many changeful and troubled moods, these quiet brown hills had not changed at all, and they were never troubled. The pulse of life only stirred subduedly in their brown breasts, and the life that lived on them was neither hurried nor obtrusive. The grey-faced mountain sheep moved quietly out of my way, and were not flustered by my puerile energy. The grouse dusting themselves on the roadside sailed on silent wing into the heather, and only one old cock, that I surprised round a corner, went off with a whirr and a warning: 'Be quick! Be quick!' And I was quick.

I breasted the last stiff brae, and from the head of it looked out across my own beloved Loch Ruighi. It lay below me, shining with its own ghostly, silver after-light, and the grey mass of the Wolf's island stood out against the shine. No other loch that I know shines with that weird self-evolved light amidst the darkening hills. But my gaze did not rest long on Loch Ruighi. Instead, it swept along the brae to where my cottage nestled below the pinewood on the breast of Cairn Rua, and what I saw made my pulse beat more quickly. One window in that small house shone like a star, and, seeing it, I knew why I had hurried across Scotland.

'The key above the door has been taken down,' I said, 'and I had better hurry.'

I went furiously down that last hill and along the shore, and in a little while came round the curve to where my own path met the road. There was no motorcar there, but as I jumped off the cycle a tall figure rose from the dyke-side and strode out to meet me.

'Archie MacGillivray, thou faithful man!' I cried, dropping the cycle on the grass edging.

'Goodness, Mr King! Is it yourself is in it?' said the surprised Archie. 'I wasna expecting *you*.' And I noticed the emphasis.

'Whom were you expecting, then?' I questioned, grasping his great hand.

'That man Leng,' said Archie, and in turn I was the surprised one.

'He is coming,' I told him. 'We left Skye about the same time, and his motor met him at Inverness—'

'I know that. He was sending telegraphs to Reroppe all day yesterday.'

'So that's it. But, first of all, is it not Miss de Burc we have up at the cottage?'

'It is so. And she milked Suzanne herself this very evening.'

'Good work! Archie, I'm pumped. Let us rest for a bit. We may not have long to wait – indeed, Leng should have been here before this.'

We sat on the grass margin below the stone dyke, our feet in the dry ditch, and Archie gave me his news in his own way.

'It was Saturday night about this time or a bittie later,' he began, 'that I came out of Hamish's door yonder and had a look across the water. 'Tis a thing that I am in the way of doing always, and in days by when I would be seeing your light I would after that be maybe deciding to come across for a talk and a smoke – or whatever was going. There had been no light at all for a long time, but this night – Saturday, as I am telling you – there was the window lighted as before, and I was wondering to myself: "Is that Mr King back, now, or is it some other one?" and that I could not be knowing without taking the bit *Nancy* across the loch. And that is the thing I did. And when I was coming up near the house I whistled a bar or two of *Farewell to Fiunary*; but when you did not come in with the turning I knew it was not you was in the house. Whoever was in it heard the whistling, and came to the door.

' "Is that you, Archie MacGillivray of Aitnoch Hill?" says she. And, "It is, ma'am," says I, "and you are very welcome"; for, though it was dark by then, I knew it was Miss de Burc herself.'

'Were you surprised?' I asked him.

'Not what you would call surprised – no' surprised at all, mind you. "Come in, Archie," she says to me. "I knew you would see my signal." She had the fire burning, and the lamp lighted, and the kettle was on the rack, and the tea dishes on the table as well. "I am very hungry, Archie," she tells me, "and there are only biscuits in the house. What have you in that basket?" "These are the scones and the pat of butter and the seven hen eggs, ma'am," says I to her that way, "and a bottle of milk moreover, for I milked Suzanne earlier in the day, and I will not be able to give you your lesson till the morn." She did not laugh at that at all, but she smiled in a way that was not like what the beginning of a laugh would be. "I well remember all that," said she, "and you have not forgotten either. We will now have a king's meal. Will you have two eggs or three, Archie?" "No eggs for me, ma'am," says I, "but I will surely take a cup of tea with you, so that bread may be broken between us in your own house." "This is my own house for a fortnight," she said then, "and after that I will not be coming back any more." And I did not like that saying. That was on Saturday, Mr King, and already she has taken to the ways of the place as if she was bred to them. She is a very inquiring young woman, and simple as well, and she does be asking the funniest questions about everything. Every day we have her over at Hamish's – in her own boat she comes too – and she having long talks with Helen, so that you would be thinking she was a girl out of the glens instead of a lady that never soiled a hand. She does be suiting the place somehow.'

A little pang went through me at Archie's words, for he implied an infinity of things that his simple words did not fail to convey. That woman up at my cottage, in spite of numberless generations of what is called gentle breeding, was a throwback to the days when Deirdre grew in beauty amongst the Dalriada hills, when Mæve was queen of Connacht and mistress of red kine and white; and I could not make up my mind whether I was Cormac, that old king of desire, or Naisi, who had thrown happiness away with both hands. Anyhow, I had lost her, and I turned Archie away from that subject.

'How did you find out that Leng was coming?' I asked him.

'From Davy Thomson, who else? He was over the hill from Reroppe yesterday asking me questions, and getting crooked answers till he told me what was in his mind. And then I wanted him to send back the good honest lie in the telegram form that he had with him, but you know the notions of honesty he has, like all Banffshire men, who will not be telling any sort of a lie unless there is no chance of being found out, and making a virtue out of that.'

'A sound honesty, too. Leng should be here long before now—'

'A hilly road he has before him, and a little thing would be delaying them motor-cars.'

'Does the lady up above know about his coming?'

'She does not. I never said a word to her, for maybe he will not be coming to see her at all.'

'I think he is. I suppose you mean that he might not be allowed to see her. How would you prevent him, you scoundrel Hielan'man?'

'Myself don't rightly know that. I would be guided by the man himself after having talked with him.'

'And it was mostly the doubt of what you might do – or not do – that brought me all the way across Scotland. Do you know, I never thought of it before, but he has probably gone to Reroppe, and will not be coming here until the morning.'

'S-s-h! Listen you to that,' whispered Archie.

CHAPTER XXV

It was the drone of a motor coming up the loch road from the west.

'He is coming, I'm thinking,' said Archie, still in a whisper. 'What will you be doing yourself, Mr King?'

'Myself don't rightly know,' I quoted him. 'Let the man guide us.'

The car, unlighted, came on, slowed down, and stopped in front of us. Night was already deepening, and we, sitting still below the dyke, remained unseen. I could make out the bulk of Leng beyond the driver, and, as he sat there after the car had stopped, I had the impression that his head was turned intently towards the light that gleamed in the cottage window above us. After sitting thus for some seconds, he got out slowly and spoke to the driver. 'Wait here, Howard,' he ordered. 'I will give you instructions later. Meantime try and get your lights going – they have been a blasted nuisance.'

He came round the bonnet of the car, and we rose to meet him. He halted abruptly and within a yard of us. 'Whom have we here?' he asked quickly.

'Archibald MacGillivray of Aitnoch Hill and Thomas King of Loch Ruighi,' I stated particularly. 'You are on the wrong road for Babylon, Edward Leng.'

The night might hide the emotion on his face, but Edward Leng was never more startled in his life. Involuntarily he started back a pace. 'This is – how – how are you here?' He barely controlled his voice.

'That does not matter,' I said. 'You might ask why I am here?'

He said nothing to that for a long time, and I waited. What his thoughts were one could only guess at – perplexed and disordered beyond a doubt, for my presence complicated things for him most grievously, and left him floundering for a fresh hold. At last he spoke in a low tone. 'Why are you here, then?'

'To meet you and persade you not to disturb a certain lady.'
I, too, spoke in a low tone.

'Yes! no doubt,' was all he said, and again followed a long pause. When next he spoke his voice was fully controlled and very reasonable, and still low-pitched.

'Look here, King, this is a private matter between us. Can I speak to you alone for a minute?'

'Certainly. I am glad you are reasonable. Let us down the road a bit.'

We went twenty yards or so down the road and halted, facing each other. The night was all about us, and I could not see his face to get a hint of the emotions that swayed him. His voice, hard-held, low-toned, almost casual, told me nothing.

'I did not expect to find you here,' he began, 'and yet where else would you be, liar and cheat?'

His words did not begin to make me angry. I had that man at the end of a tether, and would not waste anger on him.

'Your trouble, Leng,' I told him, 'is that you are not quite sure if I am a liar, and that I have cheated only you.'

'That is so,' he admitted broodingly. 'I cannot fathom you. I only know that I cannot trust you. If liar and cheat you be, then that woman up there is no better, and that is hard to believe. Yet how is she there, and how are you here? It is a damnable situation, and you will not enlighten me. You will not.'

'I could, and in a few words, which you would not believe.'

'Could not believe, and yet I want to hear.'

'Then I will lie to you. She is up there to decide between you and me.'

'And you await that decision here. It might well be, only that the decision would already be a foregone one, seeing that she is already in your house.'

'Then why come meddling? Why not take defeat gallantly?'

'Because I am not sure, damn you! But I will make sure this very night.'

'Why make things hard for her and for yourself? She is in my house, and you have lost.'

'Have I? What has been lost can be re-won. She is but a

woman after all, and any man, if he be strong enough, can win any woman.'

'You have found it so. I am glad to know your philosophy, you dog! You would be the master of the outraged. You will not see Agnes de Burc in that spirit, Edward Leng.'

'And who is to prevent me?'

Our voices had not lifted a tone in these exchanges. We spoke simply and nakedly to each other – two males without the veneer that raw man has assumed through myriad generations.

'I hold you in the hollow of my hand this night,' I told him. 'It is my turn to be high-handed, Leng. All else failing, you are always ready to try a little physical dragooning. I am prepared for that too. There is a man down the road there – speaking to your servant – and that man, big as you are, could and would tear you apart with his bare hands.'

'I might have known that you would have your bravo ready. Always you have let others fight your battles.'

'So I have. I never underestimated your strength.'

'No, and your bully will need all his strength tonight. Only death will hold me back from going up to that cottage.'

'Death! Death! You fool! That would be a simple solution. If necessary, we would kill you as we should kill a rat. Do not be fool enough to think that we would hesitate at that for a second.'

'There is the truth at last,' he said, and was silent. He must have recognized then that he was in my hands for that night. But he was so overwhelmingly possessed by his desire that he would not accept defeat. He put out a hand and laid it on my arm. 'King,' he said, almost gently, 'I must see Agnes de Burc.'

'You are more reasonable now. Why must you see her?'

'Because I must find out where I stand this night.'

'Will not tomorrow do as well? Man, cannot you give that poor girl a little respite of peace? Look you, Leng, she will be here for another ten days. Let us two go away together this night, and give her these ten days to herself. After that you can do what you please.'

'No, King! No! I have come from Skye to see her. Why

should I not see her? She has had three days to consider – the few quiet days you yourself proposed – and why should I wait longer? Granting that you can prevent me from seeing her, you are bound to play the game according to the rules of your own making.'

'Yes! But can I trust you, Mr Leng?'

'Then come with me and bring your bravo. I am not ashamed of what I have to say.'

It was not any weakness that made me yield. Indeed, from the beginning I had had no settled intention of preventing an interview, no intention other than that of showing the man that the initiative was no longer his – that I held the reins for that night.

'If you must, you must,' I said to him, 'and I am coming with you.'

We went back to where Archie waited.

'We are going up to the cottage, Archie,' I informed him. 'You will wait for me.'

'Very well, Mr King,' he agreed quietly. 'You know what is best.'

CHAPTER XXVI

The porch door was open, and Leng stepped within and knocked on the inner door.

'Come in!' cried the low-timbred voice I knew, and Leng lifted the latch and entered. I followed on his heels, and closed the door behind me.

'Is that yourself, Archie?' she said. 'Come away in to the fire and give us your news.'

She was sitting in my basket-chair, a little to the side of the open hearth and near the tidied writing-desk. She was reading, and did not lift her head for a moment. In the pause that followed her words, and before Leng spoke, I had time for a glance round the room. A peat fire was burning cheerily on the swept hearth; the hanging lamp brought out bright gleams on the dresser of blue delft; the black rafters glistened where the resin had oozed; and there was an air of comfort and tidiness about the place that I had never noticed so poignantly. Then my eyes came back to the black hair above the chair-top.

'Good evening, Agnes,' said Leng, almost casually.

Startled she must have been, but she did not show it. She laid her book on the desk, got to her feet in one lithe motion, and faced us.

'You see we have at last found you,' said Leng, striding to mid-floor. I stood just inside the doorway and said nothing.

'I see that,' she said, no tremor in her voice. 'Why are you here?'

'Where else should I be?' replied Leng simply.

She looked from one to the other of us, judging us, reading us, trying to follow the secret movements of our minds. The hungry strain in Leng's eyes must have told her all she wanted to know about *him*. My face might tell her nothing, however keenly her eyes would pry. I leant against the wall near the door, and the mask was once again clamped on the hard, lean, lined, bony crag of face that Nature had damned me with. I think it was that mask that broke her nerve at last. The stillness of her own face broke into pain, her eyelids drooped as in weariness, the long lines of her relaxed and saddened and softened, she threw her hands forward, palm outwards, and her voice quivered and broke.

'Why will you not leave me alone?' she said, and her words were addressed to me as much as to Leng. 'What am I that men should pursue me like this? I am only a simple woman looking for a little peace. Look at me. I am not moved by passion – or any desire. I do not want to be queen or slave or wife. I do not want to be the prize of intrigue or combat or desire or sacrifice. Little things content me. My desire is for peace and the slow procession of quiet days. Why will you not go away and leave me alone with what I have?'

She was looking, not at Leng, but at me, and I gave no sign. I gave no sign at all, although she had laid bare her fine and simple soul; for the least sign I might give would tell her too much. And then very suddenly a passion of anger swept over her, making her eyes blaze and mantling her cheeks with

154

colour. She stamped her foot on the boards and her hands clenched.

'Go away!' she cried. 'Go away! You men are nothing to me. I want to see neither of you – now or ever again. I am my own woman from this instant. I will not pander to any man's lust, or lose my soul for the little that any man can give. I do not love you, Edward Leng. I do not love at all – any more. Everything that has ever been in my life is wiped out, and from this moment I start life afresh. Go away!'

She threw herself into the chair before the desk, and rested her face between her hands. She had, beyond any possibility of quibble, given us our final dismissal, and I, for one, fully accepted it. It was incomprehensible to me that any man should refuse to accept her words as final, and yet Leng did that very thing. I thought that I knew the man, but the force of his passion and the case-hardening of his egotism astounded me afresh. Her words had scarcely reached him. He treated her as a child that must be gently but firmly persuaded out of a child's tantrum, that must be coaxed into a course that was the only possible one. He stepped forward – on tiptoes, too – and, I thought, was going to lay a hand on her shoulder, but at the very last moment changed his mind and placed it on the desk beside her.

'Agnes,' he said, almost coaxingly, 'you are overwrought. You must surely consider all that we have been to each other.'

'You are nothing to me,' she replied in a toneless voice, without lifting her head.

'But, my dear girl—' he began; but by then I had decided what I must do.

'Shut up, Leng!' I stopped him harshly, 'and get out of here.'

'Get out yourself, you dog!' he rasped. 'Get out, and leave me with my own.'

'There is nothing that is yours in this house,' I told him, stepping away from the wall. 'All that is in this house belongs to me.'

'Your true colours, at last!' cried Leng, straightening up and facing me. There was a new interest in his face.

'If I must flaunt them,' I gave back. 'This house is mine,

and that woman is mine, and if you do not go out of that door I will throw you out.'

'Whistle on your bully, then. Go on.'

'I will not. This is between you and me.'

'Then, by God! there is some manhood in you after all,' he cried, and the flare of battle came into his eyes.

At my first words Agnes de Burc lifted her head and looked at me, and I do not know what feelings came to her as I proclaimed my ownership. Now she got quickly to her feet and stepped between us, and her freshly acquired self-possession was again broken down. 'Why must this be? Oh! why must this be?' she said, wringing her hands.

'I will tell you that, my dear,' I said, smiling at her. 'It is because we are men and you are only a woman. And we are men in the raw, too, for things have come to that pass where you are no longer to be wooed but only to be won. Edward Leng, the oriental barbarian, will have it so, and I, the Celtic one, am no better. You have proclaimed your very splendid ideals and given us an unmistakable dismissal, but the ultimate and lustful savage in us has no use for these things. We are going to fight for you, and, notwithstanding ideals and dismissals, you will be the chattel of the victor. Now, my pagan woman, if you will stand aside, we will settle this small matter of ownership. You will be safe in that doorway, or if you want to escape the victor for the time – only for the time – you can flee while we struggle. Archie MacGillivray is down at the road, and will protect you for this night.'

She looked long at me in astonishment and curiosity as if this new side of me was beyond understanding. Then she gave a little hopeless gesture with her hands, and very quietly and slowly went across the floor and stood in the doorway of the inner room. Indeed, I was hoping that she would stand at the outer door and so have a line of retreat open to her, for, in truth, I was desperately afraid of Leng. His strength and skill I knew, and I did not know at all what I was capable of.

Leng was really a man of changeful mood, although his heavy jowl and level eyebrows gave an impression of steadfastness. I had seen him run all the gamut from god-like presumption to deliquescent gloom, and here was he now laughing with a grim merriment. His assurance had fully returned. He kicked the basket-chair into a corner, and stepped back to the open hearth.

'You surprise me pleasantly, King,' he said. 'You and I are the same man at bottom. You have proclaimed my philosophy better than I could myself.'

'I know that,' I said. 'It was your philosophy I proclaimed.'

'And your own. Come on, then, and throw me outside – or get thrown outside yourself.'

He was supremely confident. He had got me exactly where he wanted, and had no doubt of the result. Our previous encounters had always been wordy ones, and he had always been eluded and perplexed. And now I had suddenly been smitten with madness, and had voluntarily raised or lowered the battle to the plane where his youth and strength and skill gave him assured mastery. And, indeed, I myself felt much of a fool, and probably showed it. He grinned sardonically, and beckoned me forward.

'Come on, then, and throw me outside,' he said; and, before he had finished speaking, I was on him.

I summoned to my aid whatever hardihood was in me. He probably did not expect his invitation to be accepted with such suddenness. One moment I had been slouching at mid-floor, knees bent a little, arms hanging loosely, shoulders a little forward, and every muscle relaxed; next moment I had exploded on him. His confident grin was shut off for good and all. He threw up his right arm as a guard, and I caught him by the wrist and jerked him forward. At once he tried to bring his left across in a boxer's counter, but already my left arm was across his chest and against his biceps. Then my right dropped from his wrist and my long arm went round the small of his back, and for the first time we felt the quality of each other's muscles. Probably we were both surprised. As for myself, feeling the quality of his strength as he started to wrestle himself free, I knew exultingly that it was only something unforeseen that could save him from death – actual death – within the next few minutes.

For some fighting flame that had been hidden somewhere in me burst into a blaze that was somehow both exhilarating and maddening – berserk – and forthwith I set about rending apart that man's soul and body. And that thing I very nearly did, too. I lifted him off his feet and crashed him bodily on the floor, and as he scrambled up I leaped on him again, and thereafter he was never clear of my rending hands for more than a second at a time. For this was no bout of fisticuffs, but a bit of plain killing. I set out ruthlessly to smash him to death and be done with him. He never had a chance to use his acquired skill. The blows he struck or tried to strike were somehow pithless, or else my mood had toughened me to beyond feeling. Every bone and sinew in him strained under my grip, and I smashed and twisted and wrenched that splendid animal into helplessness in an incredibly short space of time. He struggled too, and desperately, but his struggles only added force to the savage mauling I gave him. I flung him against the wall, doubled him over the desk, dashed him on the floor and jerked him upright again, tore the clothing off him, thrust him into the fireplace so that one foot was amongst the scattering peats, and plucked him forth before he could burn. And then, and quite suddenly, he went limp under my hands. He was crushed against the wall, my right arm stiff as a bar at his throat, when his head sagged forward helplessly, his knees yielded, and he slid limply to the floor. I jerked him into the middle of the room, and, 'Get to your feet, you dog!' I cried. 'You cannot escape me that way.'

But head and arms hung lifelessly, and his legs trailed.

'Oh, my God!' cried an agonized voice; 'you have killed him.'

I remembered the woman. I lifted my head and looked at her, and the full weight of the fallen man dragged on my arm. I did not feel that weight, but held him as if he were a dead dog.

Agnes de Burc was in an almost crouching attitude in the doorway. I gazed at her intently and from a standpoint that was new, and, no doubt, all the fury that possessed me looked out of my eyes. She straightened up beneath that gaze, and her own eyes widened with some nameless fear. She shrank, swayed, and leant for support against the jamb of the door, her hands lifted and pressed against her breast. The utter fear, helplessness, beseechingness of her pose quenched the flame in me – and there was more in that flame than mere fighting madness – at once and for ever. And with the death of that flame I felt my breath coming in great pants, and I let Leng's heavy body drop on the floor. I managed to smile at her.

'He is not dead at all, my dear,' I said as calmly as I could for my heavy breathing. 'He is only craven. A true man would not give in till the spirit was wrenched out of him. This man's body has yielded to save his craven soul.'

She still leant against the door-post, her hands to her breast, but now she was not shrinking or afraid. She said no word, but her wide-open dark eyes stared at me wonderingly.

'Don't look at me like that, Agnes,' I said then, for I was sorely troubled for her. 'I am only your old friend, Tom King of Loch Ruighi. This thing that has happened had to be. This foolish man would not accept defeat in any way but his own. We had already made a spiritual wreck of him, and he forced us to make a physical wreck of him also. Do you not see? After destroying the dominion of his mind over yours, we also had to destroy the dominion of the senses. He would have it so. He forced me to fight him for you. But, of course, you are entirely free, my dear. Do you not see that?'

She nodded slightly, and her eyes left mine and sought the floor. Her arms dropped to her sides, but she still leant as before.

'Pull yourself together, my friend,' I besought her urgently. 'All is well with you. You are your own woman now in very truth. Life is but opening for you who are so young and have suffered pain. Rest here in this quiet place for a little time – for as long as you wish – and Archie and I will be your servants and your companions. We shall have some great days before the winter comes.'

She shook her head, but without lifting it.

'You are feeling the strain now,' I argued persuadingly. 'You will be your own calm self in a little while. Look! You will have to busy yourself. This is not as tidy a room as it might be. It will be good for you to get the place in order. I will take my-self away, and this man with me. See! He is stirring already. He will be none the worse tomorrow, and will have gone entirely out of your life. Perhaps you should not be left alone tonight. I will send Helen MacGillivray over to you.'

'No, no!' she cried, looking at me quickly. 'It will not be necessary. I shall be all right in a little – when that man is gone.'

'Then he is going now. His motor is down at the road, and so is Archie.'

Leng's senses were returning. He drew his arms back and lifted himself gropingly. I caught him, roughly enough, at the back of the neck, and he drew his feet under him, but if I had not been holding him he would have crumpled in a heap.

'I didn't know I was that rough with the poor man,' I said, with an effort to be whimsical. 'He is a bit mauled, but not beyond repair. I will say goodnight now, my lady. Are you sure that you will be all right?'

'Yes, yes!' she said, her eyes on Leng. 'Please take him away quickly. I do not want him to speak to me. Tomorrow I shall be able – to thank you for – all you have done for me.'

She looked at me with her old hooded look, and her face was very still and very white, and the old sombre quality was back in her beauty. For a time she had been unmasked, but now her soul had again retired into its secret place and gave no sign. Seeing her old poise restored, I knew that it was safe to leave her alone for the night.

She came and opened the door into the porch for me, and I shoved Leng towards it. His senses had not fully returned, and he lurched forward under my hand. At the doorway I half turned. 'Goodnight, my dear,' I said. 'Do not be fretting at all.'

'Goodnight, my friend,' she replied, and gently shut the door behind me.

Just outside the porch Archie stepped into the ray of light from the window, and took a steadying grip of Leng's other arm.

'You'll be needing a hand with him, maybe,' he said matter-of-factly.

'I am afraid the poor devil has been ill-used by someone.'

'He has so. I saw all the bad work from the window. You know I was not trusting you alone with this man, and followed you up in case he would be hurting you. My certes! I was no' needed, but glad I came. Don't you ever be getting angry with me, Mr King. I am no' a strong man at all.'

'I didn't know that I was strong.'

'I don't know yet how strong you are, but you are very strong, whatever.'

Queerly enough, we did not treat Leng as a third man of the party. We took no notice of him. He was but a hulk in our hands. The first quarter of the moon had risen over Aitnoch and showed us dimly our path to the road. There the chauffeur had turned the car, and, having got his batteries in order, switched on the lights as we came through the gateway.

'Your master,' said I, 'is not feeling too well, and we will put him in the back of the car. Take him at once to Reroppe.'

The man – that respectable English menial descended from generations of menials – whether he guessed his master's state or not, said no word, had no word to say to wild men who could so casually treat his mighty master. He hurriedly opened the door for us, and as hurriedly got into his own seat. We trundled Leng through the door and propped him in the near corner. All down the hill he had allowed us to lead, or rather to lift, him as if he were completely crippled; but now, as he leant well back, his breath came, first in a long sigh and then quickly, and he drew his feet up and his shoulders fumbled for an easier position. I leant over the door to him, and got the impression in the darkness that he was watching me.

'Glad you are feeling better, Leng,' I said. 'It is a pity that we arrived at this pass. Let us forget it.'

He said no word in reply.

'Go on,' I ordered the driver, and the metallic pulse of the self-starter started jarringly. Archie and I stood in silence till the red tail-light disappeared round the first curve.

'And that is surely the end of him,' I spoke.

'It is,' said Archie. 'Are you going back to your woman up there?'

'She is her own woman now,' I said. 'I am staying in your outside room at Aitnoch this night – and every night as long as she wants the cottage. I might even go back to Skye to complete this saga for Neil Quinn.'

'It might not be completed, my man, but you will have your

own way. Let us be going, then. I will put this bicycle in the boat, and Hamish will take it back to Barnagh in the morning. And maybe myself will take a turn across the loch later in the night to see that all is well.'

'That will be the best way,' I agreed.

And we went across the loch in the path that the moon laid down for us.

CHAPTER XXVII

It was late in the morning when Archie, clamping into the room, wakened me. 'You've had your sleep out,' he greeted me, 'and maybe you needed it. I peeped in early on, and you were like a child, for all your villainy.'

'Good morning,' I yawned. 'Do you never sleep, you opprobrious old weasel? Is the porridge boiled?'

I rolled out of bed and went to the window. The loch was brilliant under the brisk October sun. Great spaces of it were shining like a floor of silver, while here and there little wreaths of haze smoked and curled, and here and there faint catspaws of air barely crinkled the level floor. My eyes sought the little cottage nestling on the hill beyond the water, and at once I noticed the plume of smoke from the chimney.

'Yes, indeed,' commented Archie. 'Your lady doesna waste the good morning. She was up and about when I got over.'

'Oh! you have been over,' I said with interest. 'How are things?'

'Fine, indeed. She was maybe a bittie quieter than she was yesterday morning, but she was herself all the same. I took over a puckle fresh scones and cakes, and a pair of fresh eggs that Helen will be missing for your breakfast. She milked Suzanne, and I lighted the fire, and we had a cup of tea together.'

'You had, by glory!'

'We had so. And I will be leaving it to you to hint to her that her tea does be a trifle weak for my burnt palate.'

'Did she say anything about last night?'

'Never a word. She asked how you were, though, and she

hoped to see you later in the day. By the way she spoke I knew she had something on her mind, and I said to her, "You will not be thinking of leaving us, Miss de Burc?" and she said, "But it would not be fair to keep Mr King out of his own house"; and by the way she said that I knew she had another reason as well, and a bigger one. But I did not ask her to tell me that reason. "Mr King," says I, "will not be wanting you to go away, and he will maybe persuade you to stay here – for a long time"; and she could not put any more meaning into that than I had in it, whatever. We will be losing that young woman in spite of us, my man.'

'I will try and persuade her to stay, Archie.'

'You will so, and you will be using the wrong words. Now I'll be telling Helen that you are up, and I'll bring you a drop of hot water and Hamish's razor, for I don't be caring for the signs of grey in the stubble you have.'

Though Archie was older than I was by a good few years, there was not a fleck of grey in the brown mat that clothed his face.

After a breakfast of porridge, eggs, oatcakes, scones, and bitterly strong tea, Archie and I sat on the wooden bench at the house-gable, looked over the shining reaches of the loch, and smoked a philosophic pipe. And as we sat there the distant drone of a motor-car came to our ears.

That sound, not awesome, startled us very much. We jerked erect, and our eyes sought the far shore of the loch where the road ran. I was prepared to see a grey touring car, and so was Archie, for he said, ' 'Tis a dark car, anyway. See it coming out from behind the old castle. Wait till I get the glasses for you.'

He clattered over the cobbles into the house, and hastened forth again with a pair of German fieldglasses, the gift of a returned soldier, and of great use to Archie in some of his adventurous proceedings. 'You try them,' he said, pushing them at me. 'I'm no' needing them, I'm thinking.'

By this time the car had slowed down, and when I had got the glasses focused it had already halted at the gateway leading to the cottage. 'Flagstones of hell!' I swore. 'It is Lady Mary Clunas!'

'I could see that,' said Archie. ' 'Tis a bad day for us is in it, Mr King. I wonder what she will be doing to us?'

'She will be doing something, you can wager. There she is, out of the car now. Yes, by heavens! straight in at the gate and up the path. Archie, does she know who is there?'

'Fine that! 'Tis the one thing she would be knowing.'

'But how could she know? Who would tell her?'

'That young woman knows everything that happens on her policies. Am I not afraid to shoot one small cock-grouse on my own land?'

'You are a brave fellow, then, the way you subdue your fears!'

'Moreover, Davy Thomson was down at the estate office yesterday evening, and do you think he could keep any piece of news behind his teeth with Lady Clunas speirin' about you and me and our goings-on?'

'Well! Oh, well! There she is, now, up near the house, and – yes! There is a white blouse at the porch door. They are met. What will happen now? Is that hand-shaking? Is white blouse holding the door against black robes? Women of that class do not fight tooth and nail. "Is that scoundrel, King, in the house – this wicked house?" "He is not." "Let me see, then, thou shameless one!" "I will not, madam." Ha! but she is yielding. She is yielding, Archie.'

'They are both into the house, anyway,' said Archie of the eagle eye. 'What will you be doing?'

'There will be the devil to pay.'

I lowered the glasses and looked blankly at him, and he grinned at me.

'The thing you should be doing,' he said, 'is to pull over in the *Nancy* and make peace between the lot of us.'

'I will not, Archibald. Verily, I will not. Far be it from us to interfere between ladies. Let the situation develop in its own way, while we sit aloof and watch. I suppose this thing had to be, and how my respectable landlady will behave God only knows now – and we in a small short while, Archie. Damn! 'Tis a great pity, surely, that folks will not be broad-minded and generous and well-thinking.'

'Don't be saying anything bad about Lady Clunas. There is

no finer lady than herself, and she is good to all of us.'

'I know that, you old loyalist. I object only to her prudish instincts. How long are they going to be in there?'

Longer than I expected. The situation developed with painful slowness, and I grew tired of speculating on eventualities. I could not for the life of me visualize these two women together. For what seemed hours there was no movement about the cottage, and, beginning to grow anxious and even nervous, I at last jumped to my feet, and was about to stride down to the *Nancy*, when a white gleam caught my eye in the distant doorway.

'Put the glasses on them,' cried Archie, 'and give us the news.'

'They are out in the open and coming along the path. Bless my heart! I believe they are arm in arm. Is it a truce or an alliance? They are halted now, and – yes, by thunder! Archie, they are actually embracing. Oh, you women! you are a clan I do not understand. There is white blouse turned back, and black one tripping it down the hill, and in a hurry too.'

I lowered the glasses and looked at Archie.

'Soon we will be seeing what Lady Clunas has in her mind,' he said knowingly.

Presently the starting-bark of the flivver reached us faintly, and the old car moved slowly down the lochside. We expected as much. At the lower end of the loch, where the road begins to climb, it halted, and Archie whistled and slapped his knee. 'I knew it!' he cried. 'Tell me what you see now.'

'There is no need to tell you. We have been betrayed. She is opening your gate. Surely she is not going to attempt your disgraceful cart-track with her car. I thought not. Here she comes, dodging the ruts on foot, and her pace is four – at least four and a half miles an hour.'

I laid the glasses on the bench, and slowly lifted to my feet.

'What is it to be, then?' queried Archie expectantly. 'I will tell her where you will be hiding.'

'You would, or I might hide. This is my falling-off place. Great decision is now indicated, and the doing of what a man is forced to do. I am going down to meet that small cyclone.'

'And I will be watching ye with the glasses, my poor Mr King,' said Archie, reaching for them.

I strode manfully down the old cart-track, and what my thoughts were does not matter. Lady Mary saw me coming, and waited for me where the track crossed the outflowing burn by a primitive wooden bridge. She leant over the rough balustrade and looked down on the running water, and never lifted her head till my footsteps sounded on the wooden planks. I raised a humble hand in salutation.

'Peace or war, sovereign lady?' I asked her diffidently.

'Peace and war mean the same thing to you,' she said evenly, and without her usual smile. She turned and gave me her hand – gauntleted – and I noticed that her eyelids were red, and that the bonny red rose had faded from her cheeks – not faded, indeed, but lessened and receded. Yet her eyes were frank and direct as ever, though they did not hold mine for long, but looked off over the marshy course of the little stream to the brown moors closing in the valley. She leant both elbows on the low parapet behind her, and looked meditative.

'Every time I see you this airt,' I started boldly, 'I do be examining my conscience with misgiving; for, though you are very welcome, your visits are often disciplinary. What have you been hearing now, Lady Mary?'

'Something very scandalous, as you know very well.'

'Scandal travels quickly. You would not believe it, surely?'

'Would I not? I know you and your philosophy, Tom King, and I do find a scandalous state of affairs up here.'

'By heavens! you do not, Lady Mary,' I cried.

'Wait till you are accused, Tom. What I should have said was that a certain young woman has been treated scandalously.'

'That is so, but I—'

'I don't know. Perhaps you have tried to do good blunderingly, but you have shown the girl small consideration.'

'How in the world—?' I began rebelliously.

'You might have told me long ago,' she interrupted, and most illogically. 'A woman friend could have put her foot on the whole horrid business without all the melodramatic pother there was.'

This was most unreasonable, but I saw no use in arguing the case, with Lady Mary in opposition. All I said was, 'It was very careless of me'; and then, 'but how much do you know of this melodramatic pother? You have been a long time up at the cottage. What terrible confession have you forced from Miss de Burc?'

'You would like to know? She told me a good deal, my dear man, and a good deal more than you know or are ever likely to. That young woman has suffered a good deal wanting a mother, and is far too fine to be a pawn in any game that men play.'

'A pawn, indeed! Why not a queen?'

'Very well. A queen, then, and attacked by a black knight.'

'So you know. Is it not a pity, now, that she has not a white knight of her own?'

'It is; but she will find him too – some day,' said Lady Mary, with a side-glance at me. 'I am taking a hand in the game now.'

'God be good to us all!' I prayed at that.

'And my first move,' she went on, 'is to take Agnes de Burc away from here – and this very day.'

'Is that necessary, now?' I put hastily. 'Why this hurry?'

'Good gracious!' she cried. 'Have some sense of what is proper. How could that girl live up there alone in your cottage?'

'How could she not?' I cried hotly. 'Has she not Archie and myself to take care of her?'

She laughed pityingly and most provokingly. 'No use trying to explain things to you, Tom. She had already decided to go, and I am taking her now.'

'Oh! Very well.' I gave up in disgust. 'You women are a surprise to me.'

'Not half the surprise you are to us – sometimes – only sometimes, Tom. I left her packing her few things, and came round for you. I thought you might like to know, and might like to say goodbye. Will you come?'

'I suppose so,' I said in a very grudging humour. 'One cannot do less or more. It is just a terrible pity that we cannot be reasonable—'

'Tut, tut! Come along. I know what is in your mind.'

She turned and walked off the bridge, and, choking back all bad language, I strode forward to her side. We were silent till we reached the battered Ford, and I had already bent over the starting-handle when she spoke from the door. 'Do you know, Tom,' she said half musingly, 'I think you care for Agnes de Burc.'

I looked over the top of the radiator, but she was not looking at me. She was clicking the catch of the door back and forth, and seemed interested in the process.

'Do you tell me that?' I said lightly to hide discomfort.

'But you do care for her a good deal?' she persisted; and here she looked at me so that I felt my tough face colouring under that look.

'What does it matter anyway?' I said. 'I shall be saying goodbye to her in a few minutes.'

'You hid it pretty well too,' she went on, 'and I understand that you even lied about it.'

'A lie is easily told,' I evaded.

'But not so easily remedied.'

'I am not going to try, my dear lady.'

'No! You need a fresh hand in the game. You baby – you infernally lucky baby!' She spoke enigmatically, and then quickly, 'Start her up, Tom.'

We did not resume that conversation until the car drew up at my gateway. Here I got out, while Lady Mary kept her seat. She sat, one hand on the wheel and the other on the cushion and supporting her weight, leaning towards me. 'Do you know what I want you to do, Tom?' She spoke with unusual hesitation.

'No, lady; and, moreover, you will not get me to promise anything in the dark.'

'I want you to take over the lease of Reroppe.'

'Wha-a-t?'

'You can well afford to, you know.'

'Even so, there's your tenant—'

'Surely; but his lease will be broken at whatever cost to my private income. I don't suppose he will care to stay, either.'

'My dear young friend,' I began firmly, but Lady Mary had somehow acquired a habit of interruption.

'Very well. You'll remember I mentioned it, will you not? Now run up and fetch down Miss de Burc's bag – and do not be too long about it.'

So I went up the hill, leaving my decided and surprising and red-headed landlady sitting back in her seat and looking straight in front of her; and as I went I soliloquized rather gloomily. 'I suppose all adventures must end, and it is time that this one did. We cannot retain forever the high planes. Edward Leng has gone away vanquished, and now my lady – in a great hurry – is going away victorious, and here am I left to recover my old standpoint – if I can – until winter drives me to Spain. Spain! Where the castles are. Myself has built a tall one or two in that land, and that is a business that must be given up, for it is not any use at all building castles without bowers. And what is the use of a bower without a lady to nestle therein? There is only one lady that I would have nestle in any bower of mine, and to dally with that fancy is only playing with pain. Heigh-ho!'

CHAPTER XXVIII

I tapped softly on the inner door and entered. My lady's bag was lying strapped at mid-floor, and my lady herself was sitting at the writing-desk with her head lying on her arms, and she was crying sorely, sorely. At that sight I had experience of what real anguish and live yearning meant. An ache constricted my throat, and I could have wept with her – I wanted more than anything else to weep with her. I stepped forward very quietly and looked down on the blue-black hair fallen over her arms, and on the slender white neck below the hair, and it was hard enough to keep a hold on my voice as I spoke to her. 'Do not be crying, lassie,' I said foolishly. 'Don't be greetin' at all now. Sure there is nothing to cry about – nothing at all – nothing in the world worth those tears.'

The sobs that shook her ceased. She drew in a long breath, lifted her head, and turned to me. Her face was as the face of a child – smooth, unlined, innocent, and full of grief. Not the grief that convulses and twists the face – remorseful, despairing, pitiless. It was the grief of a child who has lost something world-big, and is grieving whole-heartedly for that loss. She made no sound of weeping any more, but, without ceasing, the tears welled from her eyes and rolled down her cheeks, and her voice, when she spoke, had acquired some child-like and pitiful quality that was curiously heart-touching. 'I must go away now,' she said, 'and I do not want to go.'

'Then stay here with us,' I pleaded gently. 'No one in the world can drive you away.'

'No one but myself, and I must go. Your very invitation – but you would not understand.'

'I wish that I could,' I said.

She shook the tears out of her eyes and rose to her feet, facing me. 'You must see,' she said collectedly, 'that I cannot go on living here. You think that I can live up to your level, but I cannot. I am only a simple and ignorant girl, and I am not in the least spiritual. You, with all your human understanding, are entirely of the mind. You have done a great deal for me – more than I can ever tell you – but you did it in an impersonal manner, an act of disinterested kindness for a poor human waif touching your sphere, and – going on. I cannot stay here under false pretences. If you do not understand, I am able to tell you no more or no better.'

She stopped there, and we looked at each other, and wondered.

'It is a queer thing,' said I, 'that I always understood you, and, queerer, that you have a false idea of what I am. Yet, maybe it is my own fault, and let it rest at that. You have told me nothing about yourself that I did not know. But I know more too. You possess in a high degree all the qualities that make men your slaves and your tyrants. Few men may escape the vital appeal that is in you. You are going away, and it is as well that you are going – you that think you have little you can leave in your going, and would not go if you had what we would take. And I do not know what is to happen to you in that outside world. Women like you have no respite and no retreat. Your attraction and your own personal repulsion together make up some punishment that the gods have inflicted on you since old time. These things are beyond your control, and unless you meet some strong man that you can love – little doubt but he will love you . . . I know one such man—'

'No! No! No!' she cried. 'I am done with love.'

'Perhaps you do not know love. But look you, Agnes de Burc, now that you are going away, I will not let you go with a false impression of me. I know what you are, and you shall know what I am this day. In Skye I told you that I had known the bitterness of love. That was true, but I also gave you the impression that the bitterness was of old time. My dear, I never knew what love was until I met you. I knew then, and I know now. I do love you, and it is no spiritual love either. I am as other men – of the earth; and I love you and desire you with every atom of me. That is my confession. And I am glad you are going away, for it would be terrible to have you near me – thou cold and simple woman who cannot know the passion of love! Now you know me, and let us go.'

I did not lift my eyes from her feet. I dared not. I was about to turn away, when her two strong hands caught me at the shoulders, and her eyes blazed into mine.

'Do you not see?' she cried. 'Poor simple fools! Do you not see what was driving us apart?'

Her breast was pressed against mine, and her face was up to mine.

'Do you not see,' she said, 'that I am loving you, and loving you, and loving you?'

And then she was in my arms.

If you have enjoyed this PAN
Book you may like to choose
your next book from the titles
listed on the following pages.

Alexander Cordell

An enthralling anthology of mid-nineteenth-century Wales.

RAPE OF THE FAIR COUNTRY 35p
Here begins the story of the Mortymer family, brave men, beautiful women, fighters all, whom nothing can daunt as they live, and starve, and fight, and make love, and above all slave for the cruel English ironmasters.

THE HOSTS OF REBECCA 35p
A lusty, brawling novel where strong and angry men use the cover of night to burn the hated toll-gates that bring them to the edge of starvation.

It is also the story of young Jethro Mortymer, miner by day and rebel by night, who struggles to conceal a terrible, hungry love for the gentle Mari, his brother's widow . . .

SONG OF THE EARTH 35p
Concludes the superb trilogy. Mostyn Evan and family, miners turned bargees, pray as hard as they fight, sing as passionately as they love, and face the threat of the railways with irrepressible humour and a stubbornness as hard as their native hills.

Lewis Grassic Gibbon

SUNSET SONG   40p
Book One of the trilogy A SCOTS QUAIR

Filled with loving warmth and rich humanity,
this magnificent novel, set in the years of
World War One, encompasses the life of a
woman, and the life of a people – a story to
hold all Scotland in its telling.

CLOUD HOWE   35p
Book Two of the trilogy A SCOTS QUAIR

Vivid in its panoramic canvas, this compelling
story of Scottish life continues the saga of
Chris Guthrie into the turbulent 1920s, moving from the hills of Kinraddie to the jute
mills by Segget Water.

GREY GRANITE   35p
Book Three of the trilogy A SCOTS QUAIR

This powerful and evocative novel of Scotland in the hungry thirties takes a twice-
widowed Chris Guthrie to the granite walls of
Duncairn.

'His three great novels have the impetus and
music of mountain burns in spate' – Ivor
Brown, OBSERVER

'All three novels are magnificent pieces of
writing' – J. M. Reid, GLASGOW HERALD

Walter Macken

THE BOGMAN   35p
'As quietly deceptive and as full of potential
activity as an unlabelled box of dynamite' —
LIVERPOOL DAILY POST

GOD MADE SUNDAY
  and other stories   35p
With racy speech and lively humour a rare
kind of storytelling brings the ordinary folk of
Ireland and the beauty of its countryside to
life.
Thirteen tales of drama and heroism, laughter
and tears.

Other novels by Macken in Pan are:
SEEK THE FAIR LAND   35p
THE SCORCHING WIND   35p
THE SILENT PEOPLE   35p
BROWN LORD OF THE
  MOUNTAIN   35p
THE COLL DOLL and other stories   30p